PRAISE FOR . . .

National bestselling author
Julie Kenner

"Great fun . . . wonderfully clever."
—Jayne Ann Krentz, *New York Times* bestselling author

"Shows you what could happen if Buffy got married and kept her past a secret . . . a hoot!"
—Charlaine Harris, *New York Times* bestselling author

"Smart, fast-paced . . . has you laughing out loud."
—Christine Feehan, *New York Times* bestselling author

National bestselling author
Johanna Edwards

"Brimming with escapist fun."   —*Publishers Weekly*

"More than just hilarious."   —*Detroit Free Press*

"A fresh, funny treat."   —Jennifer Weiner

Serena Robar

"Utterly charming . . . A young vampire who worries about staining her varsity leather jacket? What's not to love? I adored the book."
—MaryJanice Davidson, *New York Times* bestselling author

"Serena Robar has created a fascinating world."
—HuntressReviews.com

"A witty, emotional, action-packed read that makes Buffy pale in comparison. This fresh spin on vampires proves hard to put down."   —RoundtableReviews.com

Fendi, Ferragamo, & Fangs

JULIE KENNER

JOHANNA EDWARDS

SERENA ROBAR

BERKLEY JAM, NEW YORK

THE BERKLEY PUBLISHING GROUP
Published by the Penguin Group
Penguin Group (USA) Inc.
375 Hudson Street, New York, New York 10014, USA
Penguin Group (Canada), 90 Eglinton Avenue East, Suite 700, Toronto, Ontario M4P 2Y3, Canada
(a division of Pearson Penguin Canada Inc.)
Penguin Books Ltd., 80 Strand, London WC2R 0RL, England
Penguin Group Ireland, 25 St. Stephen's Green, Dublin 2, Ireland (a division of Penguin Books Ltd.)
Penguin Group (Australia), 250 Camberwell Road, Camberwell, Victoria 3124, Australia
(a division of Pearson Australia Group Pty. Ltd.)
Penguin Books India Pvt. Ltd., 11 Community Centre, Panchsheel Park, New Delhi—110 017, India
Penguin Group (NZ), 67 Apollo Drive, Rosedale, North Shore 0745, Auckland, New Zealand
(a division of Pearson New Zealand Ltd.)
Penguin Books (South Africa) (Pty.) Ltd., 24 Sturdee Avenue, Rosebank, Johannesburg 2196, South Africa

Penguin Books Ltd., Registered Offices: 80 Strand, London WC2R 0RL, England

This book is an original publication of The Berkley Publishing Group.

This is a work of fiction. Names, characters, places, and incidents either are the product of the authors' imagination or are used fictitiously, and any resemblance to actual persons, living or dead, business establishments, events, or locales is entirely coincidental.

PRINTING HISTORY
Berkley JAM trade paperback edition / July 2007

Library of Congress Cataloging-in-Publication Data

Kenner, Julie.
  Fendi, Ferragamo, & fangs / Julie Kenner, Johanna Edwards, Serena Robar.—Berkley Jam trade paperback ed.
    p. cm.
  Summary: Three teens—one brilliant and studious, one content to be plump, and one party girl—are selected to be groomed as supermodels by Vamp Modeling Inc., not realizing that their success depends on their becoming vampires.
    ISBN 978-0-425-21539-5
  [1. Models (Persons)—Fiction. 2. Fashion—Fiction. 3. Vampires—Fiction. 4. Horror stories.] I. Title. II. Title: Fendi, Ferragamo, and fangs.

PZ7.K3885Fen 2007
[Fic]—dc22

                            2007009702

PRINTED IN THE UNITED STATES OF AMERICA

10 9 8 7 6 5 4 3 2 1

Olivia's Odyssey

———●●———

JULIE KENNER

ONE

$\mathfrak{I}$ FOUND OUT FAST HOW WEIRD IT IS TO BE FA-mous. Even sort of famous. For one thing, you have no privacy. For another, if you happen to be famous because you're pretty, then every flaw that you thought you'd hidden is suddenly Right There for everyone to discuss. In committee. In detail. With memos and PowerPoint presentations.

Okay, maybe that's an exaggeration, but not by much. Take the photo shoot in Central Park, for example. I'd been in New York for all of forty-eight hours and had already had twenty-seven girls ask me for autographs and nine guys ask me on dates! For a girl who'd been on exactly one date in her entire seventeen years, that was pretty heady stuff.

Anyway, there I was in the playground across from the

Museum of Natural History. Sydney and Veronika were in this shoot, too, and the art director was moving us around, doing his thing with the light and the composition, and all that other art director–type stuff.

The three of us were among the winners of *Hipster Chick* and Vamp Modeling Inc.'s "Are You the Next Hot Supermodel?" contest, and our lives had been turned totally upside down. In the span of two days, we'd been whisked around New York for photo ops, makeovers, radio and television interviews, and all sorts of public appearances. (I even got to cut the ribbon at the opening of a new Sephora. *That* was fab.) The whole thing was way exhausting, totally stressful, and completely cool.

Anyway, Stan, the art director, had perched Sydney and Veronika on one side of a teeter-totter, then started to move me into the scene, pausing first to unbutton all except a single tiny button on my already nearly nonexistent blouse. The shirt flared open in the breeze, exposing my tummy, my belly button, and pretty much everything else.

Well trained by a grandmother who thinks parkas are too revealing, I automatically reached to button myself back up.

Stan just as automatically slapped my hand away. "You're my canvas," he said. "No directing the art director. *Capiche?*" He gave me a stern look, and I was just about to nod, when his focus shifted from my eyes to my forehead.

Uh-oh.

He frowned and I felt my cheeks turn bright crimson,

because I knew exactly what he was looking at. Forget revealing my belly button. The monster zit from hell had completely stolen the show.

Around us, cameras snapped and video cameras whirred. The onlookers were recording all of this for posterity. Which, of course, made my mortification complete.

"It's, um . . ." I stammered, moving my hand up toward my face.

"Stop!" he commanded. "I have to think!"

Five seconds later, I was surrounded by people. Which was actually good because I was shielded from the tourists, paparazzi, and general crush of humanity. Tanja, the personal assistant the Vamp agency had assigned to me, sidled close. As did Lisa from makeup. And Joey from hair. And Cristof from props. And Adeline from skin care (which is separate from makeup). And Daphne the photographer's assistant. Even Roger the craft services guy (which, as I'd learned the day before, means snack food) was in on the powwow.

"How could this happen?" Stan demanded, except he wasn't asking me.

I answered anyway. "I, um, get nervous, and—"

"Silence!"

"Concealer," Lisa said. "It won't be noticeable at all."

"We'll redo her hair over her forehead," Joey said at the same time.

"No chocolate," Roger muttered to himself, making a note. "Or soda."

"Don't worry," Daphne said. "We can airbrush it out in production."

"Don't worry?" Stan repeated, his cheeks turning ruddy as he focused on the volcano nearing eruption about an inch above my left eye. I shrank back as he moved in closer, finally managing to button my shirt (a total defense mechanism). "*How* am I supposed to not worry?" he wailed.

"It will be fine," Tanja said, pushing him away. "All of you, shoo." She made little waving motions and the rest of them scattered, with Stan following reluctantly while muttering under his breath. I stayed right where I was, certain I was going to cry.

"It's not that bad," she said.

"It's huge. It's like that creature from *Alien*. And it's going to burst out of my brain and take over Manhattan."

"Well if it does, maybe it'll eat Stan first."

That almost got a smile out of me. "I get them when I'm nervous. I can't help it."

"Everyone does, sweetie. You should see some of the doozies I've dealt with over the years. Some of those zits deserved their own zip codes. That's why God invented the airbrush."

"Really? But Stan—"

"Stan likes to bluster. And he wants you nervous. He wants you eating well and drinking water and sleeping twelve hours a night and all that stuff that isn't going to happen because we're going to be sending you all over the city to show off your very pretty face and sparkling personality."

"Formerly pretty face," I said, unwilling to be cheered up quite so easily. As for sparkling personality . . . well, until recently, I was quite the wallflower. But I thought it best not to remind Tanja of that at the moment.

"We'll get Dr. Lou to look at it right after the shoot," she said, referring to the dermatologist the agency keeps on staff. "I'm sure it'll be gone in the morning. At least enough to hide with makeup and hair." She gave me a quick squeeze. "And it's only your second day. Of course you're nervous. But as soon as you get more comfortable, your skin will be as smooth as a baby's bottom."

"Until then, do you think the agency would buy me a truckload of Proactiv?"

"Honey, I'm sure they would."

She cocked her head, signaling toward the trailer parked just beyond the playground. "Let's get you to Joey and Lisa. They'll fix you right up."

I sighed and looked around. Stragglers and tourists were still snapping pics, and I could only hope my zit wasn't going to make their cameras explode.

Beside me, Tanja laughed. But in a nice way. "Come on, Olivia. It's not that bad. Is it?"

I considered the question. True, I wasn't crazy about having Stan in my face, poking at my zit and making me feel lower than a bug for having one. But it *was* only one.

And I knew the way my nerves worked. Even without Dr. Lou, my skin would be clear by morning. And if I looked at the world from a zit-free perspective, I had to admit it was pretty good.

I still hadn't answered, and Tanja started to look so concerned that I had to laugh. "No," I finally said. "It's not that bad at all."

In fact nothing about this new gig as a model could be considered bad. Even Stan and his rants.

Weird, yes. Different, absolutely. Totally one-hundred-eighty degrees from the lab coat–wearing, microscope-peering job I'd figured me and my hard-earned GPA would be landing for the summer? Oh, yeah. After all I'd never once considered my toned tummy to be something that would look good on a resume or college application.

But nothing about the sitch was *bad*. Even though I was totally missing my boyfriend—and even with my forehead about to erupt like Mount Vesuvius—it wasn't bad at all.

It was going to get bad, though. The kind of bad that even Proactiv and Clearasil couldn't do a thing about.

I just didn't know it at the time. . . .

TWO

THE WHOLE FREAKY THING STARTED DURING the second semester of my junior year. My best friend, Kathy, devours every issue of *HC* (that's short for *Hipster Chick* if you're among the fashion challenged) the second it hits her mailbox.

I was at her house as usual, avoiding my grandmother and trying to do my precalculus homework, but really sneaking peeks at her brother, Damien. Damien, of course, was ignoring me—or, at least, I thought he was ignoring me—because he was only milliseconds from graduating, and what use would he have for a junior? Especially one he's known since she's worn diapers? (That would be me.)

In case you're wondering, Damien is the boyfriend I

mentioned earlier. We just hadn't reached that point yet, and I had no idea that we'd be reaching nirvana anytime soon. I knew we were fated to be together always, of course. I mean, I've known *that* my whole life. I just hadn't realized that Damien had finally picked up on the vibe.

Anyway we were all in Kathy and Damien's family room, supposedly doing our homework. Except Kathy wasn't even pretending to study. She was just scoping out the magazine. First paging through to find the candid photos of all our favorite guys. Then checking out the fashion on all the girls. I chewed the end of my eraser and waited for her to make some catty remark about an awards ceremony dress. But the remark never came. Instead she dropped a total bomb.

"Oh. My. God," she said. Just like that, too. "Oh my God, Olivia, you have *got* to read this." And she shoved the magazine on top of my notebook, so that I really didn't have any choice but to read the boxed announcement of a modeling contest sponsored by the magazine and the totally hot Vamp Modeling agency.

"So?"

"So? So you have *so* got to enter!"

I shot her one of *those* looks.

"Don't look at me like that," she said. "You're gorgeous and you know it."

I did know it, but only because people have told me so my entire life. People other than my grandmother, that is, who only throws off vague "you're very pretty" references now and then. Considering that half the time she doesn't even look at me, I figure those half-baked compliments are pretty strong stuff.

Not that I minded. I mean, it's not like I'd worked for my looks or anything. Not the way I bust my tail keeping a straight-A average. I didn't care all that much about my grades, but my grandmother would have a cow if I didn't keep up my father's legacy. He and my mom were both physicists. They died when their plane went down somewhere over the British Isles.

I'd been five at the time and the only reason I wasn't with them was that I'd come down with a nasty ear infection and the doctor said it would be stupid to take me. "Stupid" didn't really cover it, you know? At first I didn't really comprehend what was going on, but even from the very beginning, I understood that the bottom line was me living with my grandmother. And Grandmother hasn't ever been the warm and fuzzy type.

She loves me, don't get me wrong. But I think she kind of resents me, too. I mean, I totally inherited my parents' looks and their IQs. But that only makes it worse. And if I do something that "dishonors" my parents' memory (like, oh, taking drama instead of a molecular biology elective), she doesn't talk to me for a week.

In other words, my grandmother would hardly be excited about her teenage granddaughter entering a modeling contest.

Still . . .

I started to pass the magazine back to Kathy, but ended up holding on to it. According to the ad, if I was one of the winners, I'd be flown to New York, spend the summer as a Vamp supermodel, get my face plastered on a dozen magazines, and maybe even get offered a permanent job. I wasn't keen on being a model my whole life, but I'd *always* wanted to see New York. And since my grandmother mostly didn't care what I did so long as I kept my grades up . . .

I tapped a finger on the magazine as I thought about it, then did some quick math in my head. I figured the magazine had a circulation of at least five-hundred thousand. And if even twenty percent of the girls reading it entered . . .

"Do it," Kathy said. "You know you want to."

I rolled my eyes, trying to act like she was *so* not right. But the truth was, I'd spent my whole life busting my tail to keep that straight-A average. Maybe I should cut loose and do something a little fun. I mean, what could it hurt?

And New York! For a girl who'd never been outside of Texas, that's pretty cool.

Except . . .

"I've got the Cleary-Cartwright project to work on this summer," I said. The project is more like a fellowship. Kids all over the city enter, and if you're selected, you get to do work-study part of your senior year at a lab. It's way cool, very elite, and extremely competitive.

"So?" Kathy demanded. "You're only applying for the fellowship because your grandmother wants you to."

I shot her a warning look, and she raised her hands in surrender. We've had *that* argument before.

"Fine, fine, fine," she said. "But you've still got to have the project turned in before school's out for summer, right? So all you'll have to do is make the oral presentation over the break if you make it to the semifinals, and I'm sure the agency would let you fly back for that."

"You're talking like I've already won," I said, even though she'd *totally* said exactly what I wanted to hear. "And I'm hardly a guaranteed win. I mean, come on." I pointed to my chin, where el blobbo zit had popped out just that morning, courtesy of not stress, but my period. Sometimes it sucks being a girl.

And, okay, yes, this one was really more microscopic than volcanic, but I still thought it proved my point. Pretty, yes. Supermodel, no.

She rolled her eyes. "We're not going to send in a picture with a zit in the middle. Just enter the damn thing. It's not the end of the world if you don't win."

"You'll win," Damien's deep voice murmured. "Don't worry."

I turned, surprised to find him right behind me. Not surprised that he was there, but that I hadn't noticed him get up from the table and move toward me. I have an innate sense of where Damien is at all times (it's a lust thing), and I couldn't believe that my Dam-o-Meter had failed me.

I guess I really was into the contest.

Damien smiled at me, and I realized I was just staring at him like a dork. "Um, thanks."

"Just calling it like I see it. You should enter."

I licked my lips, sorely tempted. I didn't actually need summer school. And New York was totally educational. There were museums all over the place.

And I'd be away from my grandmother for an entire summer. My great-aunt Sylvia once told me I look too much like my dad, and it makes my grandmother sad to look at me. I'd been hurt and angry for a month after that. I'm mostly over it now (the hurt part, I mean) but that doesn't mean it isn't still true; if I won, chances were good that Grand-mother would let me go.

"I wouldn't know what picture to send," I said.

"I do!" Kathy slid off the couch and ran to the big desk in the far corner of her family's game room. She rummaged around and then held out a candid of me taken earlier at a chess club social. We were outside, the day was clear, my skin was clear, and the angle of the sun made my blond hair glow and my eyes seem even bluer than normal. It really was a great picture.

"If Grandmother asks, this was totally your idea."

She held up her hands. "Absolutely. I didn't even tell you about it until after I'd sent the picture off to the contest."

See, that's why Kathy and I were such good friends. She knew how to read my mind.

* * *

JUST A FEW SHORT MONTHS LATER, A CERTIFIED
letter came in the mail. I ripped it open on the front porch,
read the contents, and immediately started hyperventilating.

Damien leaned in to read over my shoulder. "Wow," he
said. "Congratulations."

"Maybe I shouldn't go," I said. He'd walked me home
from school, ostensibly to borrow a CD, but I'd noticed that
in the last ten minutes he'd never once mentioned music or the
band or anything remotely related to electronic equipment.

Instead he'd been stalling.

I considered that a really great sign. And one that made
me think that entering this contest hadn't been my smartest
move ever. For one, I'd have to get on a plane. No avoiding
that.

For another, Damien had discovered I was alive. Not
that he'd actually done anything yet, but I was more than
capable of projecting my fantasy life a week or so into the
future.

Unfortunately, according to the letter I held in my hand,
in a week or so I was going to be in New York City.

"I mean, maybe I ought to just stay here," I said.

"Now why would you do that?"

"No reason," I said, looking down at my shoes.

"It's only a four-hour flight," he said, and my insides
started to turn to water.

"Oh God." I collapsed onto the bench on the patio. I'd been thinking I should stay because of him, my fear of dying shoved well to the back of my brain where it belonged. Now it was front and center and my whole body was trembling. "Oh, God," I repeated.

"It'll be okay." His hand was on my thigh, and he gave it a gentle squeeze. "You're going to be fine."

"I know," I said. "It's not even planes. Not really." Damien had been seven when my parents died, and he remembered it better than me. But I've never much talked about all the thoughts that go through my head. Dark thoughts. About blackness and voids and a long, cold emptiness.

I shuddered and found myself looking at him, his hand now tucked firmly around my chin.

"Tell me," he said.

I opened my mouth, suddenly wanting to pour out the tangle of emotion and fear. Instead I said simply, "I'm scared of dying."

"You're not going to die," he said, just as simply.

I thought of my parents and drew in a shaky breath. "How can you know that?"

"Because if you die, I'll have to die, too. Because I don't think I could live without you." And then he leaned over and kissed me, hard enough that all thoughts of death and dying evaporated, leaving me in a warm place that I really never wanted to leave.

"Wow," I said, when he pulled away. "We should have done that a long time ago."

"Yup," he said. "But we've got a whole week to do it a lot more. After that, you can go introduce the world to Olivia Anderson. Just don't forget that no matter how much they love you, you belong to me."

I just grinned. Without a doubt, this was going to be the best summer ever.

THREE

"Liv! over here! oh my god! she smiled *at* me! Did you see that? She actually smiled at me!"

Cameras flashed all around, and I waved and smiled, striking poses and trying to shift my hips just enough that my waist looked smaller, my boobs looked bigger, and my belly button was on display.

In a mere six days, I'd come a long way from the girl with the volcanic zit who'd wanted to button her shirt. I'm a quick study, after all, and I'd learned all the tricks. And trick number one is . . . drumroll . . . *It's all about image*.

Which was why even though I'd just spent the last four hours partying my tail off in La Belle Nuit—*the* nightclub in Manhattan—and was now a sticky, sweaty mess, you couldn't tell it by looking. That wasn't sweat, it was a glow. And the way the damp material stuck to my curves was sexy, not unseemly. My skin—thanks to Dr. Lou and daily facials—was flawless. And my smile and wave? *That* was endearing me to my public.

My public. How cool is that?

Which brings me to trick number two: *The paparazzi are my friends.*

And, yes, it was a little hard to grasp the idea of me, Olivia Anderson, and "paparazzi" being in any sort of close proximity to one another. Proximity being a relative term since these dudes are *everywhere!* One pushy witch even tried to shove a camera under the stall at the bathroom in Barney's—how cold is that?

But even though they can be totally obnoxious, the first thing I heard after I stepped off the plane at JFK—after "Never wear Levi's and a University of Texas T-shirt in public again"—was that if I wanted to make it as a model I had to "cultivate a symbiotic relationship" with the camera-wielding cretins. (I have to admit, I was impressed when Marlena—from the Vamp agency—used the word "symbiotic." I've watched *8th and Ocean.* Most models aren't exactly walking thesauruses, if you know what I mean.)

I've even finally nailed the third lesson, which was the hardest one of all: *Think and act like a celebrity.* Unfortunately that doesn't mean order expensive food and wear high heels and designer labels. (Well, actually, it does. It just doesn't mean *only* that.) Instead this lesson's all about partying.

Who knew that all those parties celebs go to were shoved on them by their publicists? Photo ops. Chances to mingle and—hopefully—be chattered about in the next day's gossip columns.

After six days in Manhattan, I'd already been to over twelve parties and clubs. And—confession time—I was *so* not the celebrity those first few days!

Sure I dressed the part. How could I not, since the folks at *HC* and Vamp dressed me. But when we actually got to the clubs? Oh man, I was such a major loser! I am so not a party girl, and talking to boys is about the most painful thing ever, and they all totally expected me to mingle and flirt.

Shudder! For a geek-at-heart like me, it was almost enough to send me back home! At the very least, I expected the Rocky Mountains to erupt on my forehead!

I spent the first party locked in the bathroom, slathering on astringent and IMing with Kathy, who told me to do yoga breathing and then have a beer. I told her that was a ridiculous idea since I didn't do yoga, and my grandmother would go ballistic if I had a beer! I'm only allowed to drink on holidays, and that's a hard-and-fast rule, punishable by grounding or worse!

To which Kathy pointed out that my grandmother wasn't there, and neither was she, and I obviously needed something that would drag my tush out of the ladies' room. Even Damien agreed with his sister, which is so not the status quo! He said that even though he only wanted me seriously partying with him, if I was going to be a model I needed to start acting like one. And from what he read in the tabloids and saw on the entertainment shows, that meant being a party girl.

Point taken, but it didn't work. Not at that party or the next or the next.

At the party after that, though . . .

Well, at the next party, Tanja caught me by the elbow and parked me at a table before I could go lock myself in the bathroom. "Mingle," she ordered.

"Right. Sure. Okay." I sucked down some of the Diet Coke she'd put in front of me and tried to look interesting and sophisticated even though every time a guy came near, I was certain I'd throw up.

I just knew the contest folks would be sending me home the next morning! I mean, how was I supposed to get over this? I'm the girl who hides behind the big plastic goggles in chemistry class just so I won't have to actually look at Taylor Murchison, the totally hot quarterback who took our school all the way to State.

And, sure, I've got a boyfriend *now*. But I can just be myself around Damien. I don't have to be all flirty or fake because he loves me just the way I am. He even told me so before I left for New—

Right. Never mind. Shutting up now.

See? That's a major sign of geekiness. Rambling on . . .

Anyway getting back on track, there I was at this party, still totally stupefied by my surroundings and totally *not* loose enough to get out and dance and flirt and *whatever*. And totally worried about the whole face thing.

Since I was forbidden to escape to the bathroom, I ended up parked at the table trying to look interested and interesting. I even tried to carry on a conversation with two really cute guys, but nothing witty came out of my mouth, and they left pretty fast. (I started telling them about prime numbers and about how the clusters on the dance floor all seemed to be prime, but I guess that's not scintillating enough.)

And that's when Tanja came up with Whitney Tass, who's been a *Sports Illustrated* cover model along with being on the cover of every other magazine from *Vanity Fair* to *British Vogue* to anything else you could think of. I'd actually done a nighttime shoot with her a few hours earlier, and when she smiled and slid onto the stool next to me and told me how awesome I'd done and how great it was to see me again, I just about melted on the spot.

So when she ordered me a wine spritzer, who was I to say no? That would be rude, right? And I couldn't be rude to Whitney Tass.

Still the rules had been pretty ingrained in me, so instead of turning it down, I did the whole "I'm not allowed to drink" thing, and she did the whole "you're a responsible young lady" thing, and reminded me that I was too smart to lose control and that the Vamp agency was my chaperone and she was with Vamp and would they tell me to do something stupid?

I didn't answer that. Because logically she was *so* not on the mark. But emotionally I didn't want to sit there being a total dud while Sydney and Veronika and the rest of the winners were out on the dance floor having a great time. And Whitney did have a point. About the trip being chaperoned, I mean.

I may be a completely responsible seventeen year old, but according to my grandmother, that's not old enough to travel sans adult. But since *Hipster Chick* and Vamp Modeling swore that the whole trip would be supervised, chaperoned, and scheduled, my grandmother signed on the dotted line.

The point being, *Hipster Chick* and Vamp are in charge. And if they say to drink a white wine spritzer (or four), then who am I to argue?

So I drank. And you know what? It totally worked! Suddenly I was little Miss Chatterbox. I mean, honestly! Whitney totally took me under her wing and we cruised through the bar, mingling and talking and dancing and drinking. I was carrying on conversations and picking up threads and telling jokes and the guys were *totally* into me. How cool is that?

Majorly cool, especially since I swear I could have fired
Dr. Lou on the spot and my skin would have been none the
worse. And once I started keeping a spritzer handy, the rest
of the party stuff was a piece of cake. And so was the party
after that. And by the end of four days, I didn't even need
the spritzers anymore because suddenly I was confident,
cool, and had this acting like a celebrity thing down! So
much that I didn't even bat an eye when Marlena told me
that I was Liv from now on. Not Olivia. Just *Liv*.

Like Cher. Or Madonna. Only not so famous.

But I had to say I was getting close! In the course of a
few short days, I'd been all over *Extra, The View, Good
Morning America, Access Hollywood, Entertainment Tonight*, and even *The Insider*! Next week I was scheduled to
be on the cover of *HC* with the other girls who won the
contest, and after that I heard a rumor that *People* was doing a spread on us.

All because we looked good in clothes and had great hair
and eyebrows. Yeah, it's shallow, but it's pretty cool, too.

And the thing is, I was totally loving it. I never thought
I would. Honest! I signed up just for the trip to New York.
But this whole gig has been so amazing. Wild and crazy
and so totally not like the Olivia I was before. I mean, I'm
actually in the papers! I'm talked about on the Internet!
(Well, all of us are, but I'm included!) Damien and Kathy
have been sending me clippings, and Damien even e-mailed
me links to a ton of blogs that talk about me. (All of them

in a nice way, and Damien *swears* there are no meanie blogs out there.)

Apparently I'm a Cinderella story to some of these girls. You know, shy geek turns New York princess! And I had a whole summer before the clock struck midnight! Even Kathy's noticed my change in attitude. She says my IMs sound more lively and that she's totally jealous (which is something my fashionista friend has never said before!). I can tell she's a little miffed that I'm not IMing as much as I used to, but really, who's got the time, especially since I'm IMing Damien, too. Because he's my *boyfriend*. (Which, really, is the coolest thing ever.)

And when I'm *not* IMing or being photographed or doing an interview, Whitney is dragging me to party after party. So many, in fact, that *Access Hollywood* ran a story about us being new best buds. I never once imagined that I'd be all over the celebrity gossip wires, but there I was, on television, on the 'Net, and all over the tabloids.

Way cool.

All of which is to say that when I walked down that red carpet in front of La Belle Nuit with the flashbulbs popping and the paparazzi shouting my name, I really and truly didn't feel like a freak under a microscope. I was smiling and waving and completely in control. Honestly I totally recommend a modeling career for any girl with shyness issues. I mean, I was totally cured.

Unfortunately I was also totally exhausted, which I'd

learned goes with the territory. As Jason, the driver, held the limo door open for me, I promised myself that I'd go straight back to the hotel and just veg. It was the middle of the night, so I couldn't call, but at the least I could e-mail Kathy and Damien. And while I did that, I wanted to totally pig out on junk food, just because I wasn't allowed to do that anymore.

I climbed in, careful to keep my short skirt under control so that my rear end wouldn't end up displayed all over the Internet, getting more excited about my plan. I'd order a banana split from room service and eat every bite. Tomorrow I'd be back on veggies and fizzy water, but tonight I was going to pretend I was home.

The second Jason closed the door, I collapsed back against the leather and shut my eyes. I might be loving this whole model thing, but I was *soooo* tired. And one night off sounded fab.

I pulled my cell phone out of my tiny little purse and shot off a quick text message to Damien: *Headed bck to htl. Will email soon. Hope U R awake. XXOO.* Then I sat back and waited for Sydney and Veronika to show up. They're both pretty cool, and neither has ever said anything about the Giant Zit Incident, but I really wanted them to hurry up. Now that I'd got my mind set on forbidden desserts, I was counting the minutes until I got one!

One minute . . . two minutes . . . five minutes.

Damn.

I leaned over and pressed my face against the glass, trying to find the girls in the crowd. Nothing. But one photographer did turn and flash a shot toward the limo. I winced and hoped my smooshed face wouldn't be in tomorrow's *Post*.

I was just about to bang on the divider and ask Jason what was going on when the door opened to reveal Tanja. She's not a model, but everyone who works at Vamp is gorgeous, so she might as well be.

"You did great, girlfriend," she said, sliding in beside me. She hit the intercom button and ordered Jason to pull out. We moved slowly at first (so as to not mow down the paparazzi) and then picked up speed.

"What about the others?"

"They have other commitments," she said offhandedly. Then she leaned across me to open the little fridge and pull out an airplane-size bottle of vodka. She held another out to me. "You want?"

I shook my head. Spritzers, sure. But I hadn't worked my way up to the hard stuff. I figured I could justify wine, especially wine watered down with club soda. But vodka? No way. About *that*, my grandmother really would freak.

She studied me, then reached out and ran her thumb under my eye, presumably fixing a blob of kohl or mascara. "Here," she said, passing me a mirror. "You're a little goopy."

I tossed my head back and moaned. "*Tan*-ja," I drawled, "we're in the back of a limo with tinted windows. Who cares?"

One eye lifted in apparent surprise. "You care, I hope. After everything we've talked about, I find it hard to believe that you're willing to let yourself be seen looking less than perfect."

I sat up begrudgingly, then motioned for her to pass me the makeup kit the agency kept stocked in the limo. "Whatever. If you really think the photographers are camped out at the hotel just hoping to snap a pic of me. . . ."

She didn't pass me the case, but started handing me items. "One, they probably are camped out. And two, it doesn't matter because we're not going to the hotel."

I'd been peering into a powder compact, but now I stopped. "We're not? Oh, *man*. I'm dead on my feet. It's less than four hours until dawn. I need sleep. I need bad television. I need a gab-fest with my friends."

"Well you're not calling anyone at two-thirty in the morning. And haven't you ever heard that expression?"

I squinted at her. "What expression?"

"You can sleep when you're dead."

Silly me. I thought she was joking.

FOUR

JASON PULLED THE LIMO TO A STOP ON FIFTH Avenue in front of the most amazing building I'd ever seen. It was old—I think they call it prewar—but immaculate, and when I stepped out of the limo and craned my neck back, it seemed to disappear into the night sky.

"That's where we're going," Tanja said, and I realized she was referring to the top apartment, the penthouse. The crème de la crème of übercool addresses.

I'd been less than enthusiastic about coming here tonight, but now I was thinking that maybe this wasn't so bad. After all this was a private party—thrown by none other than Trick Traynor. Even I'd heard of Trick. Sort of a cross between Donald Trump and Paris Hilton, only richer. And classier. He was hardly ever photographed, and then only in shadows and at night. The man was mystery and money.

Most important—at least according to Tanja—he was the kind of man who could make or break an aspiring model's career. Whoever he took under his wing skyrocketed to the top. Actors, models, singers. Trick was the kind who could make a career. And even though I pretty much figured my modeling career would end where my senior year began, I was also smart enough to know that closing the door on opportunity would be beyond stupid.

"So how come you're bringing just me?" I asked. "I mean, shouldn't the rest of the girls be here, too?"

Tanja just grinned. "Honestly, Liv, modeling is a brutal world. Why on earth would you want to share?"

I blinked, taken aback. "I . . . well, you know. I mean, the other girls are—"

She waved a hand, cutting me off, and laughed. "You're too nice, Liv. But the truth is, I'm teasing you. Yes, Trick has some influence in the industry, but he's not the only route to fame and fortune. I promise you aren't being singled out. The other girls are going to be just as—" She cut herself off, cocking her head to one side as she searched for a word. "*Invested*. That's it. The other girls are going to be just as invested in the program as you are."

"Oh." I wasn't entirely sure what that meant. But my best guess was that the other girls were at equally snazzy parties in equally ritzy buildings.

"So shall we?" Her hand was on the glass, ready to tap it and signal to Jason that he could open the door and let us out.

I took a deep breath, then said a silent good-bye to my plans for banana splits and instant messaging. The door opened and I climbed out, then sashayed with Tanja past the doorman and into the marble and polished wood lobby, my chin held high, just the way the agency's walking coach had taught me.

I thought the lobby was pretty snazzy, but the elevator outdid it. No mirrors, but the metal was so shiny I could check my lipstick in it.

And the elevator wasn't even the half of it. Tanja punched in a code, and we shot straight to the top, the doors ultimately opening to reveal a crush of people all mingling in Trick's living room. The ceiling was at least three stories tall, with intricate designs carved into the wood that led up to a skylight that showed the night sky. It reminded me of the ballroom in the last scene of *Beauty and the Beast*, when Belle gets to dance with the prince who was, in my opinion, way cuter as the Beast.

I just stood there, sort of in awe, and Tanja had to actually tap my back to get me moving. I stepped into the room and noticed that pretty much everyone had turned to look at me. I swallowed and told myself not to be nervous. I'd been on display for days, and tonight wasn't any different. So I sucked in a breath and remembered my lessons—*image and celebrity.*

I could walk the walk and I could talk the talk. Hadn't I been proving that for days now? And wasn't that why Tanja had brought me here?

Feeling a little bit more confident, I moved forward, letting myself get pulled in with the crowd. A waiter arrived, and I greedily grabbed a glass of wine. I would have preferred a spritzer, but since that didn't seem to be an option, I figured I could handle the real thing.

"Girlfriend! I'm so glad you finally got here!" Whitney materialized from the crowd and gave me air kisses. I immediately relaxed. I hadn't known her for long, but just having her near made me feel better. Like I had a big sister protecting me or something.

"Don't be nervous," she said, as if she could read my mind. "You're the star tonight."

"Oh, like *that's* going to make me less nervous!"

"Get used to it, darling. You're a supermodel now. This is your life."

I took a deep breath. "For the summer, anyway."

She lifted a delicately plucked brow. "And after that?"

I hesitated, suddenly confused. I couldn't blow off my senior year any more than I could blow off college. That had always been the plan, right? Study hard, get good grades, get into MIT, and step into my parents' shoes (or lab coats as the case might be). I'd been living toward that for years. But why?

The answer came in a flash—because I didn't know there

were other options. But now I was living one of those options, and I wasn't at all sure I wanted to give it up.

Beside me, Whitney laughed. "Don't go all morbid and analytical on me," she said. "This is a party." She hooked her arm through mine, her famous smile sparkling in the lighting from the largest chandelier I'd ever seen. "Come on. I'll introduce you around."

Introduce me around turned out to be quite the understatement. I didn't go to that many parties back home in Texas, but that didn't mean I couldn't tell that this party was way, way, way, way (et cetera) over the top! In the first hour alone, Whitney introduced me to about three supermodels, a Grammy award–winning singer, a talk-show host, a guy who was up for an Academy Award, his director, and about a dozen other celebs. I met politicians, Rockettes, novelists, pundits, and a even a few scientists (who were less impressed with my modeling career than my parentage). I started out completely starstruck, but by the time Whitney slipped off to chat with someone, the whole elbow-rubbing with celebs thing was ultra passé.

Passé, that is, until I turned around and found myself eye to eye with Colin Ryband. He wasn't totally A-list yet, but according to Kathy (who knows all things celebrity), he was on his way. He'd started out as a model, morphed into a singer, and now he was the star of at least one noirish film that had a huge cult following. I figured he'd be ultra-famous in no time. I mean, the man was hotter than sin.

"You're Liv, right? A model?"

I nodded, still amazed that everyone at this party seemed to know me.

"I'm Colin."

"Yeah," I said. "That much I got."

He laughed. "You want to get some air?" And then suddenly, there I was, being guided toward the balcony by a guy who could easily end up in the next Sexiest Man Alive issue of *People* magazine! Honestly Kathy was going to just *die* when she heard that.

Although it was the middle of the summer, the balcony was cool, the breeze helped along by fans hidden among the huge potted plants and trees. Colin hooked an arm around my waist and guided me to the rail. We didn't talk, just looked out over Fifth Avenue, and I found myself amazed at how this city could still be so awake at four in the morning. At home, everyone would be asleep, the streetlights would be blinking yellow, and the sidewalks would be empty.

Below me, as if he could tell what I was thinking, a guy in a tank top and jeans walking a dog looked up. I couldn't see him that well, and I doubted he could see me, but I waved anyway.

"It's an entirely different community, isn't it?" The voice from beside me wasn't Colin's, and I looked over, startled.

"Excuse me?" I twisted around, looking for Colin and wondering how he could have slipped away without me noticing.

"The people who haunt the night. They have a different attitude. A different way of looking at the world." The man beside me oozed sensuality, and if I'd thought Colin was the most gorgeous thing on two legs, I realized now that I was sorely mistaken. Why I'd never seen this man in a fan magazine I didn't know, but right then he made the number one slot in my own personal Sexiest Man Alive list.

My mystery companion tilted his head back, his gaze shifting to the blanket of stars above us, their firelight dimmed by the ever-burning lights of the city. "I like to think we're that much closer to heaven since every night we brush the stars."

Okay, gorgeous *and* poetic. How cool is that?

Very, I thought, but that didn't mean I knew how to answer him. And my "ah ... ummmm ..." didn't have the sophisticated tone I'd hoped for.

I think my confusion amused him, because his dark eyes twinkled and his lips curved into a smile.

"You're Liv," he said.

I waited for him to introduce himself, and when he didn't, I glanced around, hoping Colin or Whitney was lingering nearby, ready to fill the etiquette void. The balcony was empty though. Apparently I was on my own, without even Miss Manners at my side.

"I'm sorry," I finally said. "You are ... ?"

"Delighted you came to my party. You've been enjoying yourself?"

"Mr. Traynor," I said, my posture suddenly straight, my

hand held out politely to shake his. "I'm so sorry. I didn't realize you were—"

"But you haven't answered my question."

"Oh." I mentally reran the conversation. "Yes. Right. Great. It's an awesome party. I'm really honored you invited me."

"Invited? My dear, you're so humble. You're an essential part of this little gathering tonight. I wouldn't possibly have considered extending this evening without you."

"Oh. Thanks." Honestly this guy's manners would put Miss Manners to shame!

"Tell me how you're liking New York."

"I love it," I said honestly. "It's so vibrant and busy. There's so much to see and do. I'm probably biased since I'm getting the red carpet treatment and all, but I think New York is the bomb."

"I'm glad you think so," he said. "And what about modeling? Has it engaged you fully, or are you simply biding your time until you hear about the Cleary-Cartwright fellowship?"

I gaped at him. "You know about that?"

"Liv, darling, information is power. Surely you can't think that someone like me would let such key information go undiscovered."

"Um . . ." *Key information?* My hope for a senior year fellowship was something a New York power mogul considered *key information*?

He chuckled and I frowned, suddenly afraid he'd been

making fun of me. "Now, Liv, don't look so nervous. We wouldn't want you to break out again, would we? Not today of all days. Your skin is as soft and clear as a peach, and that is exactly how we want to preserve it."

"Preserve it?"

He made a dismissive wave. "Isn't that what happens every time a photographer snaps your picture? The image of your beauty is preserved for posterity."

"I guess so." Honestly I wasn't sure where we were going with this, but since this was his house and his party, I knew I needed to play along. If nothing else, Tanja would be miffed if I were rude. Speaking of . . .

"Where's Tanja?" I asked.

"Inside, I imagine. Or perhaps she's gone home." Again with that amused grin. "Surely I can play the role of chaperone for a few hours? After all, it is through my efforts that Vamp Modeling has its reputation . . . and many of its top models."

"It is?" That caught my attention. Tanja had said he could make a career, but now I was wondering about the details. More particularly, was he planning on anointing me?

And if he did, then what? I'd spent my entire life planning to be some sort of scientist. I'd worked my butt off to get in my Cleary-Cartwright application, and I had a pile of college applications on my desk back home. Could I give up all my plans to be someone other people dressed, photographed, and stared at?

I wasn't sure. But deep down inside, I had to admit it was

a little tempting. At the very least, the prospect required serious consideration. Nobody smart walks away from the chance of a lifetime. *Nobody.*

Trick had already stepped through the open French doors, and I trotted in behind him. I stopped short just past the threshold, suddenly disoriented.

When Colin had led me outside, the party we'd left had been boisterous and bright and crowded and loud. Now the lights were dim and the music low, the thrum of a bass line vibrating the floor beneath my feet. What had once been incandescent light had morphed into a watery red haze, and the Beautiful People who'd been wandering around must have wandered right out, replaced instead by faceless couples (and, okay, some threeples and fourples) making out in dark corners.

The whole thing was decadent and wild and totally not anything I was prepared to deal with. I might have the supermodel schtick down, but I was still a geek at heart.

I shifted, hoping Trick could tell how nervous I was. "I, um, guess I should go," I said, keeping my voice to a whisper. "It looks like the party's over."

"Nonsense," Trick said. "The party's just beginning." He took my shoulders and turned me so that I faced him. Then he smoothed my hair out of my face and whispered a single word: "Beautiful."

I knew I should say thanks, but all I could do was stare into his eyes.

"Dance with me," he said, and he pulled me close, moving me in time with the low throb of the music.

My desperate desire to flee evaporated, replaced by another kind of desperation. I closed my eyes, lost in the sensation of his body around me.

"I'm going to do great things for you," he whispered in my ear, sending tingles all up and down my spine. "Kiss me, Olivia. Kiss me and thank me now."

I should have run away; I know that now. Instead I simply sighed, pressed my lips to his, and kissed him.

FIVE

I WOKE UP SCREAMING, THE SOUND ECHOING IN my ears as I jerked bolt upright, lost and disoriented. Then my memory rushed in, the images as erotic as they were horrible: Me kissing Trick. Trick touching me. His lips on my mouth, my neck.

A sharp pain and then the warm flow of liquid down my neck. And still his mouth. *Always* his mouth.

I remembered moaning, the pain and the pleasure of his lips against my neck almost too much to bear. My knees went weak, the room seemed to spin. My body tingled, desperate for touch, seeming to come alive even as much as I seemed to be pulling away from something.

The room got darker and darker, and the Beautiful

People who'd been tucked into corners came out to stand around us, some silent, some murmuring soft words.

I wanted to tell them to go away, but nothing was real. I couldn't make my body work, and for one horrifying instant, terror ripped through me.

Trick held me as I shook, then looked deep into my eyes. "Do you want to die?" he asked. "Or do you want the gift I'm offering you?"

I told myself that I hadn't really understood and that when I told him to help me it was because I wanted to live.

But I *did* know better. And when he slit his wrist and ordered me to drink, I didn't hesitate.

Now I was a vampire, and honestly, I had no one to blame but myself.

AFTER A FEW HOURS LOCKED IN THE SAME CUSHY bedroom (at least coffins seemed to be passé!) I wasn't blaming myself anymore. Instead I was blaming Trick, Tanja, and the whole Vamp agency!

I mean, yes, Trick had technically asked my permission, but come on! Talk about acting under duress! I've read enough legal thrillers and watched enough *Law & Order* to know *that* one just wasn't going to fly.

If they'd asked me in the first place—before we'd ever even arrived at Trick's apartment—there was no way I would have said yes. I mean, who in her right mind would choose to be a vampire? I certainly wouldn't!

They tricked me (pun totally intended), and as I paced in my locked bedroom, I rehearsed just how vehemently I was going to totally chew them out.

Except no one came.

And no one came.

And no one came.

Okay, this was getting old, and as angry as I was about being turned into a vampire (the sharp teeth were getting on my nerves and I was about to die of thirst!), I was now getting angrier about being left alone. I mean, they didn't even have the courtesy to leave me my cell phone. Or a Game Boy.

Honestly!

An hour later, someone finally came. *Whitney.*

I rushed over, relieved, angry, bewildered, and most of all, overflowing with questions.

She just held out a hand to stop me, then grinned, showing fangs as sharp as mine. "Time to party," she said, hooking her arm through mine. "Let's go."

APPARENTLY I'D SLEPT THE WHOLE DAY, BE-cause by the time we hit Fifth Avenue, it was well past sunset. Jason was waiting for us with the limo, and as he held the door open for me, he nodded, then said, "Congratulations."

I opened my mouth to answer, but didn't have a clue

what to say. So I waited until Whitney and I were ensconced in the back of the limo and turned on her. "You *knew*? You knew what Trick was going to do and you didn't tell me?"

She barely even glanced at me as she fixed her makeup. "You would have said no," she said. "Because you're a good girl, Liv. But this is the life you're meant to live. You're a model, sweetie. It's in your eyes. It's in the way you walk. And Trick just handed you this life on a platter. Nothing's going to take your looks away now. You won't grow old. You won't get wrinkles. Your hair won't turn gray. Sweetie, you won't even get another zit."

My hand went automatically to my forehead. *Preserve it,* Trick had said, talking about my perfect skin that evening. Well, at least I now knew what he meant by that.

I wanted to rage and scream and howl and kick things. But somehow I couldn't work up the energy. And the truth was, I wasn't even all that pissed about being turned into a vamp. I *should* be pissed; I knew that. But, really, the only thing that had me totally worked up was the fact that nobody had asked me. The actual being a vampire part? Well, that was kind of intriguing in an I-can't-believe-I'm-really-thinking-that kind of way.

I mean, think about it. All my life I'd been anticipating a job where I'd be holed up in a windowless room, looking down at a slide on a microscope instead of out onto the streets of Manhattan or Los Angeles or London or even BFE.

But why would I want that? Especially when I could be

out and about, being seen and photographed and making money hand over fist. I mean, get real! DNA strands might be fascinating in theory, but did I want to spend my life with my face pressed to a microscope?

No, I didn't. That had been my grandmother's dream. And, yeah, I'd been cool with it. But had anyone ever asked me if I'd *wanted* it? No, they hadn't.

For a second, the thought zipped through my mind that no one had asked me if I'd wanted the vamp thing, either. But I shook my head and freed the thought. The vamp thing was a perk, right? Never grow old. Never die.

Let me repeat that: *Never die.*

Considering all my issues on *that* subject, the idea of immortality was very, *very* appealing.

And the modeling thing? Well, that was more than just a perk. Maybe I hadn't really known it going in, but I liked the way my shyness was melting away. The way me and my chem-goggles didn't just fade into the background anymore. I liked that guys actually talked to me. And, most of all, I liked that I *finally* had the courage to talk back.

Honestly the only truly bad thing about modeling was the horrible food selection. I mean carrots and yogurt? Come on! Not that I figured the Five Basic Vampire Food Groups were going to be a huge improvement, but at least I wouldn't be eating rabbit food for the rest of my life.

Just the thought of food made me desperately thirsty, and I turned to Whitney. "I'm absolutely dying of thirst here," I said. But instead of offering me some water (or—ick!—some blood) she just laughed.

"Darling, you're already dead."

My shoulders slumped and I glared at her. "Fine. Point taken. Will you feed me now?"

She didn't. Instead she pulled me into a hug and squeezed me so tight I thought I might break. "You really are a treasure! Darling, you haven't let me down at all."

"You knew I'd be okay with all this? How? And why not just ask me?"

"How?" she asked. "By reading your contest essay. Or, rather, reading between the lines of your essay."

"Ah." The essay laid out why you wanted to win the contest and gave your basic background. Hopes, dreams, plans, grades, family. The works. Which meant that Whitney was saying that my family life was all screwed up and there was no hiding that in a personal essay. She was just saying it a lot more politely.

"As for the why," she went on. "You're too good a girl. Or you think you are, anyway. You can admit now that this isn't so bad, but ask you outright if you want to be a vampire, and you'd have gotten all prissy on us and run straight back to Texas. Wouldn't you?"

I had to give her that one. "Maybe," I said, begrudgingly.

"So just thank me, and be done with it. After all, I'm the one who got you in the program. And I'm the one who arranged the visit to Trick."

"Thank you," I said. And with those two little words, I started a whole new life. Or unlife, as the case might be.

TRICK LIVED (UNLIVED?) ON FIFTH AVENUE right cross from Central Park, and the party Whitney was taking me to was all the way down in the Battery. So while Jason schlepped us there, I interrogated her. That's me, Little Miss Scientific Method—ask tons of questions and try to figure stuff out.

"So, if you're a vampire, how did you do *Sports Illustrated*?"

Whitney laughed. "Darling, that was a night shoot."

"Oh." I thought about that. "So I'll—"

"Have night shoots, too. Yes. The agency will make sure of it."

Something else was on my mind. "Is Colin a vampire?"

Whitney smiled. "He is. And I think he likes you. . . ."

The idea gave me a funny feeling in my stomach (though it could have just been a craving for blood). "You think?" I asked, and immediately felt guilty. Because I'm in love with Damien, and I didn't have any business getting all mush-faced over some Hollywood dude.

I didn't have time to angst about the men in my life (who would have thought *I'd* ever have occasion to say, "The men in my life"?) because we were finally at the club. We got out amidst a lightning storm of flashbulbs and reporters and screaming folks who weren't as cool as us and didn't get ushered straight into the club.

I realized right away that I was different. (And, yeah, I know that's kind of a *duh* thing, but what I meant was that *everything* was different.) For one, I could see and hear everything! Whispers in corners. Guys who were commenting on my butt. Couples doing things they shouldn't be doing tucked into dark corners. It was way cool, and I stood there for a sec, just soaking it all in.

I also found out fast that whatever cute girl pheromones I might have had just from being pretty were *totally* not the bomb. Not compared to what I now had going, that is.

Every guy in the place wanted a piece of me, and they touched and smiled and stroked and bought me drinks (which I pretended to down) and pulled me onto the dance floor. At one point, I had my hands up, clapping in time with the music, as four guys did a bump and grind with me. It was hot and brutal and totally fabulous! I might have been cool yesterday, but today I was frosty! And, honestly, that so rocked.

And the best part? I never once got tired. I just kept pounding and dancing and pretend-drinking and laughing. Photographers were going crazy snapping my picture, and Whitney was right there the whole time, kind of beaming at me like a proud parent.

At one point, she jerked her head to the side, urging

me over to the bar. "Sit," she said. "At least pretend to be tired."

I bounced in time with the music. "I'm never going to be tired again! This is the most amazing, awesome, fabulous—"

She cut me off with a laugh. "It is. But you have to feed, too, or you're going to crash, and fast."

I swallowed. I'd been kind of avoiding thinking about the whole feeding thing. I knew I had to do it, but, well . . . the whole process sounded more than a little ick, if you know what I mean.

"Right. I know. Sure."

"So pick a guy." She nodded at the crowd. "You've certainly got enough good ones to choose from."

"You mean I have to . . . *kill* him?" Just the thought made me want to pass out. It was one thing being a vamp. It was another being a killer.

She laughed, and I started to feel better. "Don't be silly. Just make out. And when the time is right, take a little nibble."

"Um, won't he, you know, be a little pissed about that?"

"Not if you tell him not to be. Just look him in the eyes and tell him to forget. Trust me. It'll work."

Okay, then. I took a deep breath and started scoping out the crowd. I wished I could postpone this, but the hunger was starting to consume me. I couldn't think of anything else, not even the cell phone vibrating in the little case I had hanging from my shoulder.

Damien.

The thought ripped through my mind, and I forced my thoughts away from my possible dinners. I pulled out my phone and saw that I had about ten text messages. All from Damien, and all asking why I hadn't e-mailed when I said I would.

Gee, hon, I would've, but I was being turned into the undead.

Why did I think that answer wouldn't go over too well?

"You've got a new life now," a voice beside me said. I looked up and found myself staring into Colin's deep eyes. "Maybe you need a new guy to go with it."

My heart told me to protest, but I couldn't get the words out, mostly because Colin's mouth had covered my lips. Camera flashes lit the bar, and I knew this kiss was going to be front page on the tabloids. *The fabulous Colin Ryband has a new girlfriend.* Namely, me.

"Now you don't have to tell your boyfriend you're dumping him," Colin said. "The press will do that for you."

I wanted to slap him. Tell him to go to hell or something. But I didn't. I'm not sure why. The idea of *me* being paired with Colin? The fact that all the girls around us were looking at me like I'd just stolen the golden goose? Or was it like Colin said? "You're unique now, Liv. A model. A goddess. He's not in your league anymore."

I didn't believe that, not for a minute. Damien was wonderful. Special. He was my soul mate and always had been.

But here's the thing—did I even have a soul anymore? I was here, living in a cross between manga and *Entertainment Weekly,* and he was back in Texas living a life I could never go back to.

"It's like ripping off a bandage," Colin said. "Do it fast and clean and get on with your life."

"On with my life," I repeated, a little numb.

Gently Colin tugged my cell phone from my hand. "First, get a new number." He gave the phone a toss, and it landed in the sink behind the bar. "And don't give the number to him. For that matter, don't give the number to anyone from your old life."

My heart hitched (metaphorically anyway), but I nodded. I knew he was right. When I'd said yes to Trick, I'd said yes to a new life. And as much as I hated it, that meant saying good-bye to Damien.

I had a new boyfriend now. One who was sexy and famous and apparently adored me. Time to get with the program. And then, because I knew it was what I was supposed to do, I kissed him. Hard. And damned if it didn't feel good.

"Now go," he said. "Go feed."

And so I did. And since I was Colin's girl now, it was no trouble at all finding a guy who wanted to make out with me in the alley behind the club. I guess Andy (the guy I picked) figured it would be something to tell the guys back at the frat house. I didn't know and I really didn't care. Party girls party, right? And I was now the perennial party girl.

"Oh, man, you're hot," Andy said, running his hands over my bare back, exposed by the Armani halter I'd worn. His hips bumped mine, doing a little grind that probably would have been a total turn on if I weren't about to collapse from hunger.

His lips brushed mine, moving in for a kiss. My fangs had retracted once I'd arrived at the club and my mind had shifted to dancing. Now, though, they were back, and I felt him pull back as his tongue found the sharp tip.

"Wha—?"

I looked him in the eyes. *SShhhh.* And, just like Whitney had said, he shut up.

I'd never been Aggressive Girl, but hunger will do a lot for a vampire's gutsiness, and I pulled him close, then pressed my lips against his neck. He didn't move. Just moaned a little, and I figured that was okay. I mean, if you're dinner is enjoying the process . . .

Anyway, I bit. Oh. My. God. It tasted *sooooo* good. Better than any banana split I'd ever had and a whole lot better than those spritzers. Lights seemed to flash, and the world seemed to spin.

I drank and drank and only when he started to sag in my arms did I remember that I couldn't finish him off.

I pushed him away, breathing hard, as he curled up into a small ball.

I heard a commotion at the end of the alley and saw a

guy in a photographer's vest shove his camera into a bag and give me a wave. *Oh shit!*

The panic faded, though, just as fast as it had hit me. My back had been to the photographer, so all he would have seen was me making out with some guy. He couldn't have seen the bite.

Which meant that the worst that would happen would be that the photographer would have some hot shots of Colin Ryband's new girlfriend making out with a guy in an alley. And as mortifying as *that* might be, I also knew that the photographer was in for a surprise.

Because everyone knows vamps can't be photographed.

SIX

OKAY, SO I WAS WRONG ABOUT THE WHOLE vamps-can't-be-photographed thing. (I mean honestly! The lies Hollywood and Bram Stoker foist on people!) I suppose it's my own fault. After all, I'm a model. Why would the agency want me to be a vamp if they couldn't take my picture anymore?

Needless to say, I figured out my mistake the day after the First Feeding Incident when my picture was splashed all over the *Post* (and the Internet and a few television stations and a billion blogs!). There I was, locked in a clench with some guy identified only as "Liv's New Squeeze?"

"Apparently not," one columnist went on, "since her mystery smooch for the evening not only refused to identify himself for us, but also states that he remembers nothing of the evening. A polite guy who doesn't kiss and tell? Or did Liv's magic lips make the boy forget himself?"

I was ticked at first, but got over it pretty fast. Because apparently the whole making-out-in-an-alley thing had totally made my stock rise. Tabloid stock, that is. And the more my face showed up in the tabloids and at night clubs and bars and stuff, the more requests Vamp got for me to model clothing lines, do magazine spreads, endorse products. You name it, I was all over it.

"Just be careful when you feed," Whitney warned me a day or so after that first time. "Leave a body and we've got people asking questions. That wouldn't be good."

"Well, duh." I hadn't left a body, so why was she ragging on me?

"Sometimes it's not so easy to break away," she said, apparently reading my mind. "If you're especially hungry. Or if you're attracted to the guy. Lust has caused more than one vamp to suck a man dry, let me tell you."

"Oh." I considered that. Then I made myself a promise— only feed on guys I was *so* not interested in. And feed often.

Which, of course, was a whole vicious cycle kind of thing, since the more "encounters" I had in dark alleys the more times my name showed up in the gossip rags.

I wasn't the only contest winner who was suddenly all

over the papers, either. I saw a few of the other girls, and even though nobody specifically told me, I could tell they'd been vamped, too. Mostly, though, the agency kept us apart, hooking us up with more experienced models—both for posing and for painting the town. My guess was that the agency was afraid that if we new vamps talked together we might decide this undead thing wasn't all that great. But, honestly, I think they were worrying about nothing.

I mean, I really had no complaints. True, it was a little annoying that I had to pretend to be eating (the tabloids had a field day with the anorexia angle!). And I was kind of bummed I'd never see the sun again. But I could always go to the movies, right? And, honestly, how many times did I wake up to watch the sunrise, anyway? As for sunset . . . most people are inside when the sun goes down. So, really, what was I missing?

Not much. And the benefits *so* outweighed all the downsides. How many seventeen-year-old girls do you know who can get into the VIP room at Mondo Duomo? Not many, I bet.

Anyway, for the next three weeks, I was Cinderella to the max. Only I didn't have to leave the party at midnight . . . I just had to be gone before sunrise. Since I slept all day, I had tons of energy for partying, and after an early evening photo shoot, Colin and I would usually head to a club with Whitney and her current flame.

I'd become a huge favorite with the gossip rags, and almost every morning there was a new picture with me and whatever guy I'd claimed for dinner. *Is She Cheating on Colin?* the headline would blare, and if I hid in the shadowy corners of the clubs that night, I'd hear gossip about me, and speculation about Colin. The guys never ratted me out—how could they? All they knew was that their pictures were in magazines. They didn't remember a thing.

It was heady. Wild. Exciting.

And only one thing was wrong. (Well, other than the whole I'm-a-vampire thing, but I was finally down with that.)

Damien. I missed him. And I missed Kathy. Whitney was cool, but talking with her wasn't the same. And Colin . . . well, the man looks good, but we didn't have that connection. Not like I'd had with Damien.

I was traipsing around Manhattan with a big old hole in my undead heart, and honestly, it was starting to take its toll. I mean, sure, I could still party all night. But it just wasn't the same. I was homesick, and it was beginning to show.

Colin wasn't exactly sympathetic. "Babe, you're living the dream. Enjoy it!"

Yeah, whatever.

Whitney was a good big sister, but what could she do? I was a vamp, and Damien was just a month away from being a college freshman. Didn't sound like two roads that would be converging in a yellow wood, you know?

So I muddled on.

And then one day Whitney told me to head back to the hotel early. "These people are hanging on us like leeches. Go on. Just ignore Colin and go. The tabloids will love it."

I didn't even argue. Just got in the limo and headed back to the hotel, then up the elevator to my specially-designed-to-not-let-in-the-morning-light room. (Trick, apparently, owns a lot of New York real estate.)

I couldn't sleep (as in *couldn't*, because the sun wasn't coming up yet), so instead I vegged on the couch and watched *Dark Shadows*, this totally funky vampire soap opera from like decades ago, that I'd discovered on one of Manhattan's eight bazillion television stations.

Barnabas was just about to do something creepy when someone knocked at my door. Colin, I figured. "Go away," I yelled.

"But I just got here," a wonderfully familiar voice replied.

In a flash I was on my feet, then throwing myself across the room to the door. I yanked it open, then flung myself at Damien. "Oh my gosh! You're here! You're really here!"

"Kathy wanted to come, too," he said, after he'd thoroughly kissed me. "But she has summer school. Well, that and she's still thoroughly pissed at you."

I broke away, feeling like an absolute jerk. "I'm sorry. I'm just—"

"Overloaded and overwhelmed," he said. "I know. Whitney told us."

I blinked. "Excuse me?"

His grin spread wide. "Your friend called me. Said that I was probably miffed if I'd been reading the tabloids, but that you were desperate to see me and hated how the agency made you put on this big show of having a celebrity boyfriend and all these flings with Manhattan party boys."

"Oh." What else could I say?

He looked at me for a minute. "Well?"

"Well what?"

"Is it true?"

I took only a minute to think about it. "It's *so* true," I said. "And I missed you so much!"

I felt a little guilty, because his eyes lit up, and I'd only told him half the truth. I *had* missed him. But I hadn't not called because I'd been forced to party. I'd not called because I had a new dental condition (to say the least).

Not that I had much time for guilt, because Damien swept inside and kissed me. And kissed me. And kissed me. And oh, wow oh wow oh wow! I had *so* missed that kiss. Colin Ryband can just go take a hike because nobody—and I mean *nobody*—kisses like my boyfriend does.

It was glorious! The feel of his arms around me and his lips on mine. The heat of his body and that warm tingly sensation that I used to get when he just looked at me. It all flooded back, filling my senses and making me flush all the way down to my toes.

I was filled with lust and desperate for this guy . . . the only problem was that my body was having a tough time distinguishing feed-me hunger from oh-la-la hunger, and I had to jerk away from him, keeping my head down so that he wouldn't see the fangs that had sprouted from all of my lust-filled, hungry-for-him kind of thoughts!

"Olivia?"

"Thust a thecond," I said, since I still hadn't managed to talk around these teeth too well. I tried to think of nonhunger related things. Like Fendi purses. And Ferragamo shoes. And Manolo. And Dolce & Gabbana.

Okay, bad idea. I might be swimming in that stuff, but I did still lust after it.

Street sweepers. Local news programming. *Telemarketers.*

That did it. I turned around and flashed him a weak grin. "Sorry. Just thought that maybe we ought to take it slow, you know?"

He took my hand. "Whatever you want, babe. Maybe we should go grab some breakfast? You can spend the morning showing me around Manhattan." He smiled when he said it, and his dimple showed, and I couldn't help myself. I leaned over and kissed it.

And then, because my mind was spinning, I said, "Sure. Just give me a sec." The shades on the window had started their automatic shift to closed, and so I knew dawn was approaching. I could also tell because my head was foggy and my limbs heavy. "Just need to sit for a minute."

Part of me wondered what Damien would think. The other part was grateful that the shades were tamperproof, so he couldn't open them and accidentally fry me. The tiniest part of me left didn't care about any of that at all. I just needed sle—

THAT WAS ONE HELL OF A NAP," DAMIEN SAID.

I was slowly coming awake, and he was right beside me, all warm and snuggly. I started to sit up, but he gently held me down. My breath hitched (even though I don't actually need to breathe anymore) and I got that tingly hunger-not-hunger feeling again. "Hey," he whispered. "I'm glad you're awake."

"Me, too," I said. He wanted to kiss me. But I couldn't let him. I was *ravenous,* and there was no way I'd be able to control myself . . . or my fangs. One kiss, one caress, and I'd be fanging all over the place. He'd see, he'd run . . . and that would be that.

No. He just got here! I was so not letting him get away that fast.

If I could just get a quick bite (so to speak), then I could have quality time with my boyfriend.

Which meant heading to a club. Which meant taking Damien.

But so what? He was here now, right? And sooner or later everyone would know that Colin was out of the picture. If nothing else, the PR hounds would have a field day.

"What is it?" he said, eyeing me suspiciously.

"I've got to get moving," I said. "I shouldn't have slept so long. I'm supposed to do face time at this restaurant and then a club and then—"

"I get it," he said. "We're going out."

"You don't mind?"

He stroked my cheek. "I just want to be with you."

I sighed. Is he wonderful or what?

WE WENT TO RUE TWENTY-EIGHT SIMPLY BECAUSE it wasn't one of my usual hangouts, and I didn't want to bump into Colin or any of the other girls from the agency. The music is intense, the kind that goes right through you, with the bass line pounding in your gut. It sucked us in the moment we walked through the front doors, and Damien tugged me onto the dance floor and didn't show any signs of letting me escape.

"The VIP list," he shouted over the din. "Did the guy at the door know you were coming?"

I shook my head. "I get that a lot now."

"Very cool," he said, and I couldn't help beaming. My boyfriend thought I was cool. *That* was the absolute definition of cool.

What *wasn't* cool was the fact that I couldn't manage to get away from him. Not that I wanted to get away, but by definition, I had to leave if I was going to sneak off and seduce my dinner in an alley. And I *so* needed to eat. On the way there, Damien had asked if I wanted to stop somewhere for a bite, and I'd wanted to absolutely scream! Of course I wanted a bite!

That answer, however, wouldn't have gone over real well, so I'd made up some excuse and dragged him straight to the club. Now I was trying to think of an excuse to sneak away.

My brain must have been fuzzy from hunger, because it took me a good forty minutes to come up with the lamest (and best) excuse—that I needed to go to the bathroom. (In my defense, vampires *don't* need to go to the bathroom, so that particular excuse wasn't high on my list anymore.)

Anyway I was just turning around to drag Damien to a table near the bar where he could wait for me when Colin showed up. "What the hell are you doing here?" he shouted, grabbing my arm.

"Hey!" Damien said, jumping to his feet. "You want to let go of my girlfriend?"

"Your *what*?" Colin stared him down. "Do you have any idea who I am?"

"Sadly, yes."

I could practically smell the blood that was about to be spilled, and since it was Damien's, it didn't make me hungry; it made me sick to my stomach. I had to do something, so I jumped between them and tried to make peace. "Come on, guys. This really isn't the place for a scene, you know?"

"I think it's the perfect place," Colin said. He glanced to his right, and I saw the crowd snapping away, digital cameras and camera phones all aimed right at us.

Great.

I shot Damien a look that I hoped indicated how much I wanted him to just be quiet. Then I took Colin by the elbow and pulled him aside. "He's just here for a few days," I said, whispering.

"So what are you saying? This is just temporary? You're showing around a friend from the old hometown. Ho ho ho?" He sneered. "Come on, Liv. The guy is in my face and he's snaring *my* press."

My temper flared. Not at him, but at me. What was I doing lying? Damien wasn't just here for a few days! He was here to stay . . . at least if I had anything to say about it.

But more than that, I didn't want Colin. I never really had, and now that Damien had stepped in, I actually had the guts to say so. "We're over," I said.

"Good. Go tell the bastard to get lost."

"Not him and me. You and me. *We're* over."

He jerked his head back, and for a split second I wondered if I'd slapped him without realizing it. Then his eyes fired. "What did you say?"

"You heard me." I stood up straighter, pulling courage from the heavy bass beat.

I watched the fury fill his face, my hands fisted at my side as I told myself not to be scared. What could Colin do?

Nothing, as it turned out. He just bared his fangs and narrowed his eyes. "He's not like us, Liv."

I almost tossed back something mean, like "he's not like you." I didn't, though. Colin was okay; he just wasn't the guy for me. And I felt proud of myself for being so reasonable even though I was about to attack a passing waiter because I was starving to death.

Apparently Colin didn't appreciate my magnanimity, though. After I shrugged, he glared. "This isn't over, Liv," he said. And then he brushed past me and headed for the back of the club. Since that was the perfect opportunity, I signaled to Damien and then pretended to follow. In reality I was scoping out the crowd. Two minutes later I'd found dinner, and a minute after that we were in a dark alley.

"Wow," the guy said. "I mean, I think you're so hot, and you're here, and I'm—"

"Shut up," I said. And I bit him.

Heaven.

Honestly if I'd gone any longer, I think I would have shriveled up or attacked Damien on the dance floor or something.

I drank and drank, the overpowering stench from the nearby garbage Dumpster not even making a dent in the glory that was me finally getting to feed.

Even though I could have happily drained him and then moved on to a dessert boy, I shoved him aside well before he'd passed any sort of critical point. It was hard, though, and I remembered what Whitney had said about losing control if I was extra hungry or if I was turned on by the guy. Thankfully I wasn't at all turned on by this guy! And even though I was hungry, I was more afraid of leaving Damien alone in the club. I mean, what if Colin decided to go back in there?

I put my hands on my knees and took a couple of deep breaths, trying to pull myself together before I went back inside. One breath, two breaths . . .

Okay.

I stood up, ready to go in, and found myself face to face with Damien.

Uh-oh.

"So," he said. "Are you going to tell me what's going on? Or do I have to guess?"

I took an involuntary step backward, my head shaking, not in denial but in disbelief. "Honestly, Damien, it's nothing."

He pointed to my dinner, now sleeping like a baby next to the garbage. "Nothing?"

I bit my lip. "Please. Not now. It's just . . . it's just . . ." My shoulders dropped. I couldn't think of a single lie. "Honestly, Damien, it's not what you think."

"Really?" he said. "Because what I think is that you're a vampire. And you just had *him* for dinner."

SEVEN

OKAY, THEN. APPARENTLY IT *WAS* WHAT HE thought. That's why I totally love this guy. He's so smart. And he really pays attention to me. I mean, how many guys pay enough attention to their girlfriends that they would actually put all the clues together and come up with "vampire" as the right answer?

I'm thinking not many.

"So you're really okay with this?" We were back at the hotel, and I was kind of gaping at him. Because I couldn't quite believe that he wasn't freaking out. I mean, did I know how to pick great guys or what?

"Quit asking me that," he said, with a laugh. "I'm okay. I already told you."

"Yeah, but *which* part are you okay with? Me being vamped? Or me living at night? Or me being famous? Or me—"

He shut me up with a kiss. "All of it," he said. "I'd love you no matter what, but . . ." He trailed off with a shrug.

I, of course, started to freak out.

"But?" I squeaked. "But what?"

He gave me a sheepish grin. "But I kind of like the night-life thing."

I shoved at his shoulder. "No way!"

The grin became even more endearing and his dimple deepened. "What can I say? It's intriguing. I mean, *you* thought so, right? And if it's good enough for you . . ."

He trailed off, then pulled me close and kissed me. Kissing was okay, but we couldn't get too serious. No biting or nipping or anything like that because, you know, I didn't want him to accidentally become dinner. But even so, we had a lovely time doing the make-out thing until I passed out when the sun came up. I'm not sure what he did while I was out cold, but by the time I came to at sunset, he was dressed and ready to go clubbing.

I found a barely-there red dress, did my makeup the way Lisa had taught me, and took his arm, thinking that we looked so hot it would be a miracle if we didn't burn up the town.

* * *

𝔍 WAS RIGHT ON WITH MY *HOT* ASSESSMENT. Over the course of the next few weeks, every tabloid and gossip columnist in print and on the Net pretty much said that we were the hottest thing in the city.

Damien was totally eating it up. While I slept, he spent the days researching the coolest places in town. I think the boy was surviving on four hours of shut-eye a night, and he was wired. He was also sexier than sin, and not going further than basic making out was killing us both. I'm not even talking sex. Because, you know, I was probably the only vampire in the world who was still a virgin. But that didn't mean I wasn't totally down with the idea of serious making out. Except that we couldn't. Even though we really, really wanted to.

We hadn't actually talked about it, though. The not making-out thing, I mean. Because what can you say? "I love you so much I'm going to leave you if I can't have you"? Something told me that wasn't the best approach.

For the most part, we were so busy club hopping and fielding the media that the lack of make-out time wasn't an issue. I actually felt a little bad for Colin. Because not only was the press all over Damien, but they seemed to have forgotten about Colin. I'm not sure why my stock was so high, but for some reason the fact that I'd dumped him seemed to have put his career in the toilet.

Rumors were he was being turned down for parts, and his latest record wasn't doing nearly as well as the first. All of which had to have really pissed him off, especially since Damien had already been called by no less than two producers who wanted to know if he was interested in being screen-tested for an upcoming flick.

Damien—because he's the love of my life—told them no. That would require flying to L.A. And since I couldn't go with him (too many shoots), he said that he couldn't go, either. Is that love or what?

And, yes, "too many shoots" was an understatement. I swear, I was being photographed so much it's a miracle I didn't go blind from all the lights!

At any rate, we were totally the golden couple for weeks and weeks. We were both loving it, except that we weren't.

Or at least I wasn't. I wasn't sure about Damien because I hated to ask. He was so good in the spotlight, and he was always up for another party or another dance or another cuddle in a dark corner.

So how could I tell him that being golden was starting to get on my nerves. I mean, nobody wanted to be with me, Olivia Anderson. It was all about Liv the Model. What could Liv do for them? Could Liv put in a good word with a producer? Could Liv get them into a party? Could Liv get a few extra seats to the latest Broadway show?

In high school, I used to feel sorry for Bethany, the head cheerleader, because she was so popular that I figured she couldn't tell if people liked her for her or for the fact that she was Bethany. Now I knew how she felt. Other than

Damien and, maybe, Whitney, I was surrounded by people and still felt like I only had two friends in the world.

But like I said, I didn't want to say anything because why rain on Damien's parade, you know?

So to the clubs we went, hanging with all the people that didn't like us for us but for what we could get them. The whole situation was exhausting. All the more so when we'd bump into Colin, and he'd spend the evening trying to get the media's attention and then shooting me killer looks when they didn't seem the least bit interested in him.

I wanted to tell him to get a life, but he couldn't. Because he was undead. Just like me.

Honestly I was becoming positively morbid!

In fact I was so lost in my morbidness that I didn't even notice that Damien was cutting our nights shorter and shorter. One hour before dawn. Two. Three.

When we ended up back at the hotel at 12:45 on a Friday, I finally clued in that something was up.

"I'm just tired of it," he admitted when I asked him. I held my breath, afraid I was reading too much into what he was saying.

"Tired of what, exactly?"

"The party scene. I mean, it's fun and all, but it's getting kind of old. Don't you think it's getting old?"

"Oh, man, *yes*. So old it's moldy!" I couldn't help smiling, I was soooo happy he felt the same way, and I snuggled up close and we vegged on the sofa and watched really bad movies on the Sci-Fi channel. Now *that* is a perfect date.

"I want to take you to Central Park," he said. "I want to ride in one of the carriages."

"We can do that," I said.

But he wasn't finished. "I want to go shopping on Fifth Avenue. I want to take the Circle Line harbor tour."

I swallowed. "That's a sunset cruise, isn't it?"

He turned to me, his eyes full of sadness. "Damn it, Olivia, I want us to watch sunrises together. I want us to watch sunsets together. Hell, I want there to be fireworks, you know? I want us to *really* be together."

I stood up, suddenly angry. "If this is about sex—"

"It's not," he said. He shook his head, like a dog shaking off water. "Or, yes, it is. But not just that. I love you, Olivia. I want to be with you. And it's tearing me up that we can't."

"You don't think I'm ripped up, too."

He closed his eyes and rubbed his forehead. "I know you are. I'm just venting. I'm just—"

"Are you leaving me?" I whispered.

"No," he said. But there was something in his voice. And I knew that Colin had been right all along. We were from different universes and there was no way this was going to work.

I wanted to cry, but I couldn't. I don't know if other vamps can, but my tears stopped flowing the second I was changed. "No," I said. "Don't think that. Not yet. Not until we try everything."

His forehead creased. "What are you—?"

"Just wait," I said. "Don't move."

And then I was gone, desperately hoping he'd wait for me, even as I hoped just as desperately that my last ditch solution would work.

Darling, I thought you liked it," Trick said.

"I do. I mean, I did." I licked my lips. "Now I want my life back."

"Your life? But you have a fabulous life!"

"I have a lie," I said. "And a bunch of people who want to watch me but don't care a thing about me. If I break up with Damien tomorrow, no one's going to tell me they're sorry or try to comfort me. They'll just wonder about who I'm going to hook up with next. Either that or they'll decide they don't care about me at all anymore."

He looked at me, his head tilted a little to the side. "Well, well. Little Liv has grown up."

I lifted my chin. "Olivia, if you please."

"Why don't you simply have Damien join our exclusive club?" he asked, as if we were talking about the weather.

For half a second, I entertained the idea, then I shook my head. I'd bought into the whole vamp thing because I'd been seduced by the fame as much as I'd been terrified of dying. But the whole thing was wrong. *Off.* And I didn't want to do that to Damien.

I didn't say all that to Trick, though. I just shrugged. "I want him to see sunrises and sunsets. And I want to see them with him." I looked him in the eye. "I want a *life* with him."

"Olivia, I just don't know if it's possible." He sat, suddenly seeming more like a father than a vampiric mogul. "There are rumors about daywalkers. Cured vampires. But I've never met one."

"I want to find out."

"Hard to do if you're working as a model."

I nodded. "I know. I want to go home. Here, Damien's just second to me being rushed from party to party and shoot to shoot. At home, we can be together."

"Are you sure?"

"I don't think I've ever been this sure." I wanted my old life back. A life where people were interested in me because I was smart or witty or could do trigonometry in my head.

"Then good luck," he said.

And that was that. I'd been expecting some big moment out of *The Godfather.* Or at least that I'd have to bare my fangs and threaten to go to the *Post* and reveal all. But none of that happened.

I was free.

I could go home.

But I was still a vampire.

* * *

My RELATIVELY GOOD MOOD FADED THE SEC-ond I got back to the hotel. Why? Because Colin was there.

And this wasn't just the bad feeling you get when your ex bumps into your current boyfriend. No, this is the kind of bad feeling you get when your ex is a vampire and has trapped your current boyfriend, intent on draining all of the blood from his body in a fit of violent revenge.

Needless to say, I was a little hysterical.

"Colin! Stop!"

He stood in the middle of the room, furniture broken and twisted around him. These men had fought, but unlike in the movies, the bad guy had won. Now Colin held my boyfriend glassy eyed in his arms. Colin's own eyes burned with hate, and he lifted a lip in a sneer. "Stop? I don't think so, babe. The way I see it, this guy ended my career. I think it's only fair I end his life."

I realized I was shaking my head, back and forth and back and forth, while I kept repeating, "No, no, no, no!"

"No what?" he sneered. "No, don't kill him?" He pushed Damien away and pretended to consider. "Hmm. Maybe you're right. Maybe I should keep him around for food."

"Olivia," Damien whispered, his voice so soft I could only hear it with a vampire's ears. "I love you."

"Awww," Colin said. "Isn't that sweet? A little too sweet

for my blood. I think I'll just finish him off now. Like candy. No sense saving what I can savor now."

I screamed, and he sank his fangs again into Damien's neck. Damien's already pale skin seemed to grow translucent, and I rushed forward, not certain what I was planning, but knowing that if nothing else I had to save the man I loved.

"Too late," Colin said, dropping Damien to the floor. "You can go after me or you can say good-bye to your boyfriend. You don't have time to do both."

I hesitated for just a second, wanting revenge, but there was no way I could leave Damien. And as I knelt by his side, Colin yanked open the door and vanished into the hall.

"Damien," I whispered, frantically shaking him. "Please don't die. Please, you can't die."

"Not scared," he whispered.

My eyes seemed to well with tears, but I knew it was only an illusion. "I'm not, either," I said. "Not anymore." I was so sorry. Sorry for all the choices I'd made. And sorry most of all for the choice I was about to give him.

I licked my lips and silently begged forgiveness for what I was going to do. "How badly did you want to see that sunrise?" I asked.

His smile was weak, his laugh thin and liquid. "I can live without it," he said.

"Yeah," I said. "You can *only* live without it." I bared my fangs and slashed my own wrist. "Drink."

And so help us both, he did.

* * *

LET ME JUST SAY THIS: ALL THAT TALK ABOUT how the whole vampire suck-fest thing is a majorly erotic experience? All true. Every single word of it. You might think it would be gross (and I guess in theory, it really is) but when Damien drank from me, it was as if I'd fallen into a tunnel of lust with the one guy in all the world that I loved. Trust me on that, because I'm so not describing the details. Those yummy tidbits are mine alone.

It was late by the time his strength returned, and we slept through the day, then awakened together to look out on his first night as a vampire.

"The lights look brighter," he said.

"Everything looks different," I said. "You get used to it."

He paused, then kissed me. "Thank you."

"For turning you into a vampire? I was half-afraid you'd hate me."

"That honor goes to Colin, although I suppose I ought to thank him, too."

I cocked my head. "Why?"

"Would you have done it if I hadn't been, you know, about to die?"

I shook my head. "Never." I paused. "Would you have asked me to?"

"No." He didn't say any more, but I understood. If he were still mortal, it wouldn't have worked out between us.

No matter how much we might have wanted to stay together, the threads were already starting to unravel.

"We'll be okay now," I said, but it came out a question even though I hadn't meant for it to.

"Yeah," he said with conviction. "We will."

I took one final look at the skyline of Manhattan, then turned away. I went to the closet and pulled out my suitcase, tossing it carelessly onto the bed.

"Are you going somewhere?"

"*We're* going somewhere," I said. "Home."

"Are we?" he asked, but the smile on his face told me everything I needed to know.

"I miss your sister," I said. "I miss not being the absolute center of attention. I even miss my grandmother. I'm not sure how we're going to explain this or make it work back in Texas where pretty much everything shuts down after midnight, but I want to try."

"We'll figure something out," he said. "At the very least, we can work the all-night shift at Taco Bell."

I laughed. "Actually I was wondering if the folks at Cleary-Cartwright would be interested in a lab intern who can only work nights." I thought about what Trick had told me. The rumors of day-walking vampires. "Someone with a particular interest in studying the properties of human blood," I added.

"You never know, babe," Damien said, with a laugh. "It's worth a shot."

He gathered his things, too, and we headed for the door and pulled it open—only to find Trick standing right there.

"Going somewhere?" Trick asked.

I lifted my chin. "We're going home. You said I could go home."

He laughed, the sound rich and throaty. "Darling Liv. Who ever heard of an honest creature of the night?"

"You bastard!" I spat.

"Tsk, tsk, Liv," he said. "Such language. And after I arranged for your heart's desire." He gestured toward Damien. Then his mouth curved into a tight smile.

"You arranged— You, what?" I stumbled over my words, confused.

"He sent Colin to turn me into a vampire," Damien said, apparently faster on the uptake. He looked Trick in the eye. "He figured that you'd stay. If I was a vamp and could keep up with your nightlife, then why wouldn't you stay here?"

"Why not indeed?" Trick said. "You love modeling. It's opened up the world to you, Liv. Made you see yourself in a new light. Given you new confidence. Don't deny it, Liv. You know it's true."

I swallowed, because Trick was saying back to me all the things I'd told myself so many times.

Damien reached out and took my hand, sharing his strength with me.

"Go back inside," Trick said congenially. "You two enjoy your wonderful suite. Tomorrow night Vamp will have a shoot for you, and after that, you can take Damien around to the clubs for a few more photo ops." He cocked his head, examining Damien. "I'll have Maurice come by and take a few Polaroids of Damien, too. I think he just might be useful in the Vamp stable. Not top male model quality, but there's a certain flair. You two would be quite the couple."

"Sure," Damien said flatly. "That would be great."

Trick looked at him hard, as if he were sizing him up. "No hard feelings?" he finally asked.

"I'm alive, aren't I?" Damien retorted. "At least, in the walking-and-talking sense of the word."

"Good boy," Trick said. To me, he said, "You've got yourself a smart man. I think you should listen to his counsel."

"Right," I said. "Sure."

He gestured to the door. "Go on now," he said, as we stumbled inside. "Enjoy yourselves. Young love is so touching." His smile thinned. "By the way, I wouldn't recommend going out this evening. You two need to rest. And just to make sure you do, I'm changing the elevator code and locking the fire exit doors." He bowed, then swept away, leaving Damien and me looking after him, with a sense of both relief and trepidation.

"Think he doesn't want us making a run for it?" Damien said.

"Yeah," I admitted. "That's the impression I get."

I headed back inside and flopped on the couch, not at all

sure how I felt about anything at the moment. Damien sat on the coffee table and held his hands out until I took them. "Is he telling the truth? Is this really the life for you?"

I sighed, wishing it wasn't all so hard. "Everything he said is true," I admitted. "But at the same time the whole thing has been so unreal, you know? Pretend friends, pretend emotions. I felt like I wasn't me. Just a glossy eight by ten."

"So what do you want to do?"

"I want to go home," I admitted. "Like we planned. But how can we? They're not going to let me go. I'm too hot right now. And I stupidly told Trick I wanted to leave, and he just turned around and trapped me. And then tricked me into trapping you."

"We could just go and not look back."

I looked pointedly at the door. Trick owned the building, and he'd flat out told us he'd locked us in. We weren't going anywhere.

"Tomorrow then," Damien said. "We can sneak out. Catch a cab. Run away."

"They'll come after us," I said, my voice little more than a whisper. "Oh, Damien, I'm so sorry. I never meant for this to happen. I never meant for you to end up trapped here with me."

"Hey," he said, moving to the couch and hooking an arm around my shoulder. "The point is I *am* with you. And we will survive. Somehow we'll make this work."

I leaned against him, soaking in his comfort despite feeling like a rat in a cage. A sharp knock at the door startled me, though, and I jumped up, suddenly scared.

"Liv? Are you in there? Open up!"

Whitney!

I raced to the door and pulled her in. Her face was a mix of anger and sympathy. "I'm so sorry, kid," she said. "You, too," she added, with a nod to Damien.

"Sorry?" I repeated. "But you're the one who pulled me into Vamp in the first place."

"Because I thought it would be a fit, darling. But we're friends now, aren't we? And if you want out, then I want to help you."

"How do we know we can trust you?" Damien asked, which, under the circumstances, was a perfectly reasonable question.

"You don't," she said. "Here." She passed us a huge shopping bag, and I opened it, pulling out men's and women's jeans and T-shirts that were most definitely *not* designer. "Put them on. The hats, too. The elevator code is nine-two-four-five-eight."

She turned to go.

"Wait!" I cried. "He'll just come after us."

"Maybe," she said. "Or maybe if you're already gone I can convince him it's not worth the trouble to try to find you. Maybe I can point out that if he goes after you, you might get pissed off. Convince him that once you're out of

New York, it would be easy for you to go to the press. Start rumors about Vamp Inc. Maybe even about him. Because, you might, right?"

"Oh, yeah. Absolutely I might."

"That's what I thought," she said. She paused at the door and turned back to us. "Keep a low profile until you're out of the city. Trick has people everywhere. And if you're caught, I was never here."

"Thanks, Whitney," I said. "You're a good friend."

Her smile wavered, but her eyes stayed dry. She was, after all, a vamp. "You, too, Olivia. Now go."

We waited until she was off the floor, then changed into the ratty clothes. The code key worked just like she said it would, and although Damien had been a little nervous that it was a trap, I trusted Whitney. I'd been wrong about one thing, at least: I'd made one real friend during my modeling career.

We skulked out of the hotel, found our way to the bus station, then bought a ticket for some small town in New Jersey I'd never heard of. It didn't matter where, just that the bus got in well before sunrise.

Not long after, we were settled on the threadbare seats of the Greyhound bus, looking pretty much like everyone else in our thrift-store duds. A far cry from the limos and Versace I'd gotten used to, but I didn't care. Damien and I might be vamps, but we were together. We were free.

And right then, that was all that mattered.

Veronika's Venture

JOHANNA EDWARDS

ONE

"Do you know how many calories are in that?" my mother demanded, staring in horror at the mammoth-sized banana-nut muffin in my hands.

I gave her a big, sassy smile. "I can't even count that high," I said, and then took an enormous bite.

I was being snarky, yes, but I couldn't help it. Before this whole it-started-as-a-joke-but-now-I-might-actually-become-a-model thing happened, Mom never cared about what I ate. She never cared that I was a size twelve (borderline fourteen).

Mom used to fill my bookshelves with feminist tomes like *The Beauty Myth* and *Reviving Ophelia*. She would clip out articles with titles like "Love Your Body at Any

Size" and tuck them into my L.L. Bean backpack. Now she seems bent on getting me to join the anorexia squad.

Funny how things change.

Mom shook her head disapprovingly. "Not to mention, that muffin is loaded with carbs."

"True. But the carbs are what make it taste *sooooo* good," I said, savoring another delicious mouthful.

We were sitting in the departure's lounge at Cleveland Hopkins International Airport, killing time until my plane took off. I should have left twenty minutes ago, but the flight was running four hours behind schedule. Talk about annoying. I'm not the most patient person by nature, and I have a crazy short temper (hey, it's true what they say about redheads). Sitting and wasting time is *not* my forte. My one-way ticket to NYC's LaGuardia airport was burning a hole in my pocket. I was dying to get out of town. If I had to stay here too much longer, listening to my mother drone on about fat grams and calories and waist-to-hip ratios I was going to scream. Fortunately it was nearly time to head back to the gate.

"Veronika." Mom sighed. She'd been sighing at me a lot lately. "If you keep eating that way, your modeling career is going to be over before it starts. Here." She reached into her purse and pulled out a no-carb, Splenda-laced candy bar. "Why don't you try this instead?"

I resisted the urge to remind her that I was going to New York to become a *plus-sized* model—and that skimping on calories might actually *hurt* my career in the long run. Instead I just kissed her good-bye, gathered up my things, and headed toward the security checkpoint. "Thanks for the snack, Mom. I think I'll save it for the plane ride." I took the candy bar (and, really, I use that term loosely—how can something with no fat, no sugar, and no carbs be classified as candy?) and shoved it into my Fendi Zucchino Baguette.

God, I love that purse.

It's chic and stylish, with its familiar double F logo and sleek black trim. Actually I think the color is called Nero. Or maybe Noir? That would make more sense. *Noir* is the French word for *black,* after all. (See, Madame Dupont. I did retain something we learned in French I.)

I scratched my head and tried to remember what that modeling rep, Iris D'Abruzzo, had told me. She'd given me the Fendi handbag two weeks ago, as a sort of "Welcome to the fold!" gift. Even before I'd left Millew, Ohio (which is affectionately known as Mildew to its 3,129 residents), Iris had kick-started my makeover.

"You can't traipse around New York with that Kate Spade knock-off," she'd said, eyeing my faux designer backpack purse with disdain. And she didn't stop there. "I know this is going to sound harsh. But your nails look like they've been through a paper shredder, your hair's in desperate need of a deep conditioner, and your feet are screaming out for a pedicure. Don't get me wrong. You've got tons of potential, Veronika, but you definitely need a little refinishing work."

Despite the fact that she was kind of snooty, I really loved Iris D'Abruzzo. I loved her bluntness, her sophistication, and most of all, I loved the fact that she'd handpicked me as one of the fifteen winners of the Vamp Modeling Inc. and *Hipster Chick* magazine nationwide search.

In other words, Iris was largely responsible for me getting this awesome opportunity in the first place.

And to think, it started off as a dare.

Allow me to explain: A few months ago, *Hipster Chick* started running ads for its annual model search. It does this every year (hence, the "annual" part) but it's never once come to anywhere in Ohio. Usually the casting calls are held in only the biggest cities: New York, Chicago, Los Angeles. Which I've always thought was kind of stupid. After all, girls in New York have tons of opportunities to be discovered as models. If *Hipster Chick* really wanted to find the "next hot new face" then wouldn't they branch out a little and hit some of the Flyover States? Apparently someone at the magazine had the same idea I did. Lo and behold, this year they decided to blanket the country, holding open casting calls in nearly thirty cities. As luck would have it, one of the locations was at the Cleveland Mall, which is only a forty-five-minute drive from Millew. I swear to God, half the girls at my high school decided to try out.

Kerry Malone, the queen of the "Bitch Brigade" (my secret nickname for the group of snotty girls who dominate the social scene at Millew High), took it upon herself to organize a carpool out to Cleveland. She went around to all the juniors who had cars, begging them to take part. Since I'm the proud owner of a 1997 Dodge Neon (the lamest ride in existence, but it gets me from point A to point B), Kerry asked if I'd be willing to join the fun.

Well, sort of.

"Missy and Jamie and Lisa need rides," she'd said, referring to three of her bestest buds. "Would you mind playing designated driver? *Pretty please?*" She'd batted her eyelashes at me, a move that presumably worked better on guys than girls. It's not like I swing that way, if you catch my drift.

"You could drop us off at eleven o'clock and then pick us up later. We won't be more than two or three hours, tops. You could catch an afternoon movie while you're waiting."

This infuriated me. I was so mad, my face practically turned as crimson as my hair. "Or I could try out," I said simply, trying to play it off like it was the most normal suggestion in the world.

"Get real, Veronika," she'd said, rolling her eyes. "This is a modeling contest we're talking about here. Not a casting call for *The Biggest Loser*."

That did it. "I've got more model potential in my pinky finger than you have in your entire body."

"Considering your pinky finger weighs more than my entire body, that's not too shocking."

I'd walked right into that one. I wanted to smack myself.

Kerry dissolved in a fit of laughter. "You can't compete with girls like me. You'd get laughed right out of the building."

I tried to stay calm. There was no sense in letting her have the satisfaction of seeing how upset I was. "Well, how about we let the judges decide? Or are you afraid I might be too much competition for you to handle?"

Kerry flipped her hair over one shoulder. "You *can't* be serious."

"Oh. Why not?"

"Because. That's, like, ridiculous. You're a nice girl but, well, you're a fatty boom batty. And fatty boom batties sit this stuff out."

I'd been facing this kind of thing for the past couple of years. There seems to be this general consensus, this ill-formed misconception about any girl above a size ten. It's like if you're the least bit overweight, you're not allowed to participate, not allowed to be a full-fledged member of society. You have to sit out not just modeling competitions, but dating, sex, parties, sports, and well, life in general. You're supposed to hang out on the sidelines, letting life pass you by while the thin and glamorous claim their rightful places in the spotlight.

I have never been one to sit on the sidelines. And I've never been able to resist a dare, which was exactly what I took Kerry's comments to be.

She'd turned on her heel to go, but I grabbed on to her

left shoulder. "Like I said. Let's let the judges decide next Saturday. I'll be there. And I'll win the whole damn thing. . . ." I added.

And that's exactly what I did.

Much to the shock of Kerry Malone, and pretty much everyone else at Millew High, I'd made it to the semifinals. Iris D'Abruzzo took an instant liking to me, and she and the other judge passed me through to the next level, and then the one after that, and before I knew it I was on my way to New York with a lucrative modeling contract.

Or, at least I would be, if my plane ever took off.

A FEW HOURS LATER I FINALLY ARRIVED AT LA-Guardia. As the plane taxied down the runway, I felt a burst of excitement. I knew I should be playing it cool, adapting the part of the unaffected, aloof supermodel-in-the-making but I couldn't suppress my glee. *I'm here! I'm actually here, primed to spend my summer in the Big Apple!* I caught a glimpse of the famed New York skyline through the plane's tiny window.

Wow.

I know it sounds cheesy, but the image literally took my breath away. It was so striking. I had only traveled about five hundred miles to get here, but somehow Millew, Ohio, and Kerry Malone and my overbearing mother felt like they were light-years away.

After I got off the plane I headed over to The Coffee Beanery in the main terminal. That was the designated meeting place. Iris had instructed me to "grab a cup of coffee and wait for me there. I'll have someone get your stuff from baggage claim. You won't need to worry about a thing."

As I strolled into The Coffee Beanery I spied two girls seated at a table. They were sipping drinks and chatting animatedly. I could hear the words *Vamp models* and *Hipster Chick* floating over from their conversation. I quickly glanced in their direction. They looked to be around my age. One was blond, one brunette, and both were insanely thin, with long twiglike legs that seemed to stretch on forever.

Yup. They had to be the other winners of the competition!

I slung my Louis Vuitton carry-on tote (another gift from Iris) over my shoulder and approached their table.

"Let me guess. You guys are here for the model search, right?"

They broke into simultaneous grins. "Sure are!"

I spied a stack of *Hipster Chick* magazines sitting on top of one of the tables.

"I'm Veronika," I said, extending my hand.

"Hi, I'm Laura," said the blonde. "With a U."

"Huh?" I asked, staring at her in confusion.

"And I'm Lara, *without* a U," the other girl supplied.

They giggled hysterically. This was obviously an inside joke that amused the hell out of them.

"That's cute," I said, not really meaning it. It was kind of annoying, but I didn't want to make enemies right off the bat.

"Uh-huh," Laura With a U said, not seeming very interested in me. She turned back to Lara Without. "Anyway, sweetie, I've had three espressos since my plane touched down. I'd better go pee or else I'll be burstin' on the car ride into Manhattan," she said, dashing off.

"Are you one of the handlers, Veronika?" Lara Without asked, leaning her elbows against the countertop. She stirred her cup of plain black coffee. I noticed an uneaten protein bar sitting on the table in front of her, and I almost laughed. My mom would be so proud.

"No, I'm one of the model search winners—I took first place in the Cleveland finals. I'm here for the *Hipster Chick* assignments." I gestured toward the stack of magazines. "Just like you guys."

Her eyes got huge. *"Really?"*

"Yup. Really."

"I just . . ." She seemed shocked. "Well, you're certainly tall enough, I guess. Even though you're not, you know . . ."

It was obvious "you know" was code for thin. *Ouch.* It was Kerry Malone and the Bitch Brigade all over again.

I snagged a chair from a nearby table and pulled it over.

I figured I would join them, even though Lara Without hadn't invited me to sit down. Big mistake. I should have kept my distance. They started in on me the second Laura With a U returned from the bathroom.

"Veronika is a model search winner," Lara Without said, raising her eyes in an exaggerated fashion.

"Oh," Laura With said. "*Oh.*"

They exchanged a glance. Then the barrage of questions-slash-insults started.

"Not to be nosy, but is your hair always this frizzy?" Lara Without asked. "Or is it the humidity? In case you didn't know this already, New York in the summer is like a steam room at the gym."

Before I had a chance to answer, Laura With a U said, "How old are you, anyway? I thought this was a competition for teens. You look like you're in your twenties."

I smiled. "I know I look really sophisticated and all, but I'm only seventeen years old," I said, my voice dripping with sugary sweetness. "Imagine that." I was determined not to let them get to me. I didn't know why they were being so nasty. I was a plus girl. It wasn't like we were going to be competing for the same job assignments. Did they honestly feel threatened by me?

"You're like a ghost," Laura With a U said, looking me up and down. She lightly touched my forearm. "Have you ever thought about hitting the tanning bed?" She snickered and nudged Lara Without.

I've been hearing this all my life. When you're super pale, people are constantly saying, "Why don't you get a tan?" Hello, Captain Obvious. Do they not realize that pale people burn? I couldn't tan to save my life (I get a wicked sunburn every time). At my high school, tanning is pretty much the number one after-school activity. It's stupid, really, because these girls spend countless hours, not to mention mega bucks, in the tanning bed just so they can show off their bods to absolutely *no one*. (Unless they're strippin' down to do the nasty with a guy. But that's another story.)

It's not like Millew is the Mecca of beachwear. We're nowhere near the beach, and very few people even have outdoor swimming pools, considering the climate is less than tropical.

I flipped my long red hair over one shoulder and gave Laura and Lara my most confident smile. "Funny you should say that. My pale skin is part of what got me to New York in the first place."

It was true. When I'd gone to the audition at the Cleveland Mall, the first thing the modeling reps commented on was my complexion. Not only am I totally zit-free (despite the fact that I never, ever use acne products and don't even regularly wash my face) but my skin is smooth as silk. Plus, with my striking red hair and snow-white skin, I really stood out. (Of course, when you're the only big girl in a room full of borderline anorexics, you stand out by default. But whatever.)

Even Iris D'Abruzzo, who normally had a critique for everything, couldn't find fault in my skin.

"It's stunning," she'd told me. "Being pale is your ace in the hole. You have a really unique look, and that's what's hot right now. The day of the perfect Christie Brinkley blondes is a thing of the past."

I wasn't entirely sure who Christie Brinkley was so I Googled her. I felt pretty damn stupid when I realized she was one of the biggest models of, like, *ever*. But you have to understand, before winning this competition I knew next to nothing about the fashion industry. I didn't know Gucci from Gautier, Heidi Klum from Heidi of the Swiss Alps. I'd never even seen an episode of *America's Next Top Model*.

Before Laura/Lara could respond, Iris D'Abruzzo came bustling into The Coffee Beanery. "Hi, girls," she said, embracing us with quick hugs. "Ready to see your new apartment, gals?"

"Hell yes!" Lara Without said, clapping her hands together. "I'm dying to check out our digs."

"Great," Iris said. "We just need to wait for one more person and then we can go. In fact, he should have cleared customs by now."

He? Customs? I didn't follow her. As far as I'd known, this contest was only for girls—*American* girls, at that. Why was there a *guy* coming in from a foreign country? It didn't make sense.

"Have any of you seen Dex Holcombe, by chance?" Iris asked, pulling out her Razr and flipping it open.

I heard someone gasp. Laura/Lara, I guess.

"Who's Dex Holcombe?" I asked.

Lara Without stared at me as though I'd just sprouted horns. "You're kidding, right?"

I shook my head. I'd never heard of Dex Holcombe in my life.

"He's only the hottest male model *in the entire world*. He's been in every major runway show—not to mention every magazine you've ever heard of."

"Or *never* heard of," Laura mumbled. "Our Veronika doesn't seem too up on the fashion world."

Lara Without snorted. "Dex is with Vamp Modeling, but I guess you didn't know that, either."

I shrugged, trying to appear cool and unaffected. It didn't work.

"Jesus, Veronika, didn't you study up on this before you got here?"

"Yeah! How could you not know he's with Vamp?"

"I vaguely remember reading something about Dex being with the agency," I lied. "But I chose to focus on my own modeling career, rather than obsess about other people in the industry."

I thought this was a pretty valid point, but Iris D'Abruzzo disagreed.

"It pays to know your competition," she said, punching numbers into her stylish Razr phone.

"Well, to be fair about it, Dex isn't technically my competition. Being that he's got a penis and all." I shouldn't have said it. I knew it was obnoxious and kind of lame. But I was at a loss for what to say, and I wanted to appear edgy and indifferent. But Iris was annoyed. And she kind of had a right to be.

"There's no need to state the obvious," she scolded me.

Lara Without giggled. You could tell she found all of this hilarious.

"What I meant is that you need to know what's going on in the modeling world. You need to know the key players. And not just the people you're directly competing with, either. Know all the big name models. Study them. Watch what they do. And learn from it."

I nodded. "You're right. I will." And I meant it. But it must have come off wrong, because Iris took it as sarcasm.

"I'd advise you to take this a little bit more seriously, Veronika. Otherwise you'd might as well pack your bags and head home now."

"No, no, of course not." I rushed to clear things up. "I'm totally committed to this. I'm just a little jet-lagged at the moment. I'll be back on my game as soon as I rest up."

"You got jet lag from a quickie flight from Cleveland, huh?" Lara Without mumbled under her breath. "I thought you only got that when you, like, switched eight time zones or something."

"No lie. Veronika, you need to get out more. You're downright sheltered, girl," Laura With a U said.

I ignored them. "So tell me more about Dex," I said, as Iris D'Abruzzo stepped out into the concourse to make a private call.

They began rattling off a list of Dex Holcombe's many accomplishments. In addition to being a male model extraordinaire, Dex was a regular fixture on the party scenes. Plural. He had a VIP pass to every hot club in New York, Los Angeles, Milan, London, Paris, and Tokyo.

"Those are *his* cities," Lara Without informed me. "I saw him being interviewed on *Access Hollywood* a few weeks ago. He was at some party with Lindsay Lohan, and he was talking about how he divides his time between those six places, with occasional stopovers in South Africa and Miami. He's such a world traveler. I think he's done runway shows on, like, all five continents."

I didn't have the heart—or the nerve—to tell her that there were actually seven continents.

"And he owns a private jet, I heard," Laura With a U chimed in.

"I read online that he's thinking about buying a Greek island! The guy burns money."

Geez. Talk about glamorous. How had I not heard of this

guy? True, I wasn't a pop-culture expert—I'd rather read a book than watch *Laguna Beach*—but I wasn't completely naive, either. I knew all the major stars, even if I couldn't tell you who was bonking who.

"Dex models for all the biggest designers," Laura With a U said. "He's the most sought after male model in the world."

"And he also had a bit part in that JLo video last year. God, he looked so hot in that."

"I heard he's dating Paris Hilton."

"Nah. She's skankified. Dex wouldn't sink that low. I read on Page Six that he hooked up with some gorgeous European princess."

Princess? Were they kidding?

"They're, like, practically engaged. Which makes him royalty," Lara Without said, raising her eyebrows for emphasis.

I wished Iris would hurry up and come back so she could settle the argument for us.

"No, I swear. He's with Paris."

"Uh-uh. Dex Holcombe is, like, practically engaged to this royal chick from Madagascar or some other European country."

Before they could finish the argument, a guy's voice cut them off. "You're both wrong. Dex Holcombe is single."

As if on cue, the three of us whirled around.

There, in the flesh, was the most gorgeous guy I'd ever

seen in real life. He had light blond hair, a strong, chiseled jaw, and the most beautiful blue eyes I'd ever seen in my life. He reminded me of Jensen Ackles, the actor who plays Dean on *Supernatural*. Only taller and with a better build.

"And, for the record, Madagascar is an island off the coast of Africa. It's not part of Europe," he added.

I stared, in complete shock. Was this guy for real?

"Hi, I'm Dex," he said, ignoring Laura/Lara and turning his attention toward me. He reached forward and took my hand in his, holding it for a few seconds. "Veronika James, right?" he asked, smiling brightly.

I stood there, dumbfounded. Dex Holcombe—*the* Dex Holcombe—knew my name? Up until two minutes ago I hadn't even realized he existed. Yet this god of a man had heard of *me,* some utterly unfamous size twelve (borderline fourteen) chick from the middle-of-nowhere Ohio?

It seemed too good to be true.

TWO

I͟T WAS.

"How do you know who I am?" I asked, giving him my friendliest smile.

"It's written right there." He pointed to the Louis Vuitton tote hanging from my shoulder. Sure enough, my luggage tag had flipped around, revealing the place where I'd written Veronika James in big swirly letters.

Lara Without started giggling. "It's not like Dex is familiar with your work or anything. Speaking of which, have you done any modeling before?" she asked. "I was in *Seventeen*'s prom spread last year," she boasted. "And Laura has worked for *Elle Girl* and *Justine*. Have you done, like, any stuff for Lane Bryant?"

I felt my face flame up. "Nope, no modeling experience. Not yet."

Laura With a U snickered. "That's odd. I wonder if it's a bad sign?"

"It's a good sign, if anything," Dex said, sounding bored. "It means Veronika has a lot of potential if she won without ever having any experience. Do you guys know where Iris is?" He looked annoyed.

"I'm right here, love!" Iris said, rushing over to greet him. They exchanged air kisses. "Dex, your car's out front." She handed him a set of keys.

"What have I got this time? Don't say a Mercedes."

"No. *God* no," Iris assured him. "It's a BMW Seven Series. Is that okay?"

Dex shrugged and jingled the keys. "Sure. See ya," he said, waving good-bye. And then he was off.

A few minutes later, Iris had shuffled us off to the parking lot where a black stretch limo picked us up. "We've already collected your luggage," she said, ushering us into the car. "We've got a tight schedule. Waiting for Dex slowed us down a little, so we really need to hustle."

"Where was Dex?" Laura With a U asked. "Did he fly in from Paris or something?"

"Tokyo," Iris said, fiddling with her cell phone. "He's been in Japan for the past week."

"Japan!" I sighed. "That's so awesome."

"Yeah, Japan has a piping hot fashion scene," Lara Without said knowingly.

"Maybe we'll get to go there someday," I said dreamily. I've been dying to visit Japan ever since I first watched the Scarlett Johansson movie *Lost in Translation,* which is one of my all-time favorite films. I've seen it so many times I practically have it memorized.

"I wouldn't count on it," Iris said, as the limo pulled out of the airport parking lot. "Japan's a tough market to crack. They're extremely picky about what kind of girls—and guys—they'll take. Dex works everywhere, of course. But the Japanese have major requirements about body type. Anything above a two doesn't fly. Laura Balcombie," she said, gesturing toward Laura With a U, "could probably go there. She's thin enough. But you guys are pretty much SOL."

Lara Without was visibly shaken. "I'm not that big," she said. "I'm a size two."

"Honey, you're a four if I've ever seen one," Laura Balcombie said viciously. Uh-oh. They were turning on each other already.

"SOL," Lara Without a Thin Enough Body repeated. "What does that mean?"

"Shit out of luck," Iris informed her, as the limo was absorbed into the Saturday afternoon traffic.

It wasn't a kind way to put it, but as I was quickly

learning, the modeling business didn't pride itself on coddling people.

It's a good thing I've got a pretty thick skin.

WE WERE STAYING IN AN APARTMENT ON THE Upper West Side. It was beautiful in a classic sort of way, although it wasn't nearly as posh or spacious as I'd pictured it would be. I guess it was true what they said about New York City—space was at an absolute premium. Even Vamp Modeling, despite being one of the biggest agencies in the biz, wouldn't spring to stash us in a huge luxury penthouse.

I was rooming with a waiflike redhead named Mindy March. Mindy was from Peachtree City, Georgia, and she had an adorable Southern drawl. Her speech was peppered with *y'all*'s and quirky phrases like *fixin' to*. Such as, "I'm fixin' to take a nap," which she said about five minutes after we arrived.

Mindy was super nice, which made me thrilled. After the hellish airport meeting and limo ride into Manhattan with Laura/Lara, I was happy to see a friendly face. Laura B. and Lara Without were going to be rooming together. Which seemed fitting.

"Before you get too comfortable, let me talk to you for a minute," Iris said, motioning Mindy over. She gestured for all of us to sit down on the couch. "I don't mean to over-whelm you right off the bat, but we do need to get a few things out of the way."

She began laying out ground rules. They were the exact opposite of what I expected.

"Basically there are no rules," she said, and waited for it to sink in. Nobody said anything. I think we all thought she was joking. "We do require that you show up for all of your appointments and photo shoots, of course. But aside from that, anything is fair game. If you want to stay out all night drinking and snorting coke, we don't care."

"Snorting coke?" I repeated. "You're joking, right?"

Iris smiled. "Maybe a little bit. I don't want to steer you guys down the wrong path or anything like that." She winked in exaggeration. "But I was using the drugs example for emphasis. I just wanted to show you that no matter how far you take things, we're not going to narc you out to your parents."

Lara Without said, "You realize most of us are under-age."

Laura B. nudged her, as if to say, *Shut the hell up! Don't remind her!* Which was kind of dumb, considering Iris had all of our personal information on file—from our Social Security numbers to our bra sizes to our dates of birth.

"*All* of you are underage," Iris told us. "But so what? You're not little kids. You can handle yourselves. But we're not going to be your watchdogs, your babysitters. You're free to come and go as you please. You're free to do whatever—and *who*ever—you want."

We sat there in silence for a minute, taking it all in. Then Mindy asked, "When you came to visit me in Georgia, you mentioned the New York club scene. You said we'd all have VIP passes. Is that true?"

Iris nodded.

"Even though most clubs only let you in if you're over eighteen or twenty-one. We can still go?"

"That's right."

"My mom's gonna die!" Mindy exclaimed.

Mine would, too. If I were stupid enough to tell her, that is.

"When she hears about this," Mindy continued, "she'll be so jealous she'll lose it. It was her dream to be a socialite in New York," she explained. "When Iris told her about all the fun stuff I'd get to do with Vamp, she was green with envy."

Whoa.

So Iris had told Mindy's mom we were going to be living it up while in the city? That was mad crazy! When Iris spoke with my parents a few months ago, she painted quite a different picture. She'd informed them that Vamp Modeling would keep a close eye on us, that we'd be well taken care of. "We'll give the girls a safe, professional environment where they can learn and grow as models as well as people," is how she'd put it.

Even then, it had kind of reeked of BS. At first my parents seemed skeptical. But Iris spoke to them for nearly an hour, telling them all the positive reasons why they should let me go to NYC. In the end, my mom and dad had bought her story hook, line, and sinker. And, as much as it pains me to admit it, so had I.

I wonder why Iris told Mindy March (and, presumably, her mom) the truth, but then kept me in the dark? I know it would have been weird to spill the beans to my parents, but she could have pulled me aside or something. She could have casually given me the 4-1-1 at the same time she was giving me the complementary Fendi Baguette and Louis Vuitton carry-on luggage. I understand lying to my folks, but why lie to me?

Maybe it was the fact that I give off this serious vibe some of the time. I don't know why people often get this impression of me. I guess it's because I love reading and politics and I'm not obsessed with the whole *Us Weekly*, who's-banging-who kind of life. But that doesn't mean I don't love to cut loose from time to time. (Okay, most of the time. But, honestly, in a place like Mildew, Ohio—where having your own car immediately gets you on the A-list—how much partying can a girl do?)

Maybe Iris had sensed that my parents were horribly nervous about letting me come to New York in the first place? After all, it was Iris's little talk "Veronika will be chaperoned around the clock" that convinced my parents to let me do this in the first place.

"Trust me, you're going to have the time of your life here," Iris predicted, patting Mindy on the arm.

"I hope so," Mindy said, giving her a big smile.

After Iris had finished going over our rules (or lack thereof) she handed out our schedules.

"You guys have pretty similar schedules for the next couple of days," Iris told Mindy and me. "You'll both be rising bright and early tomorrow morning—around five o'clock, I think—and then it's off to a full day of go see's."

I had heard the term before, but I wasn't exactly sure what it meant.

Mindy seemed totally clued in. "Go see's! I can't believe we're starting those tomorrow. God, this is so surreal."

Iris went on to explain that a "go see" was sort of like a casting call for models. We'd visit various clients—designers, magazine editors, etc.—and let them size us up and then decide if they wanted to hire us.

"Oh!" Iris said, smacking her head. "I'm being such a dumb ass here. I completely forgot. You guys have been selected to do the *Hipster Chick* winter formal spread. You'll get to wear these gorgeous gowns. You'll be working with Trudie English, who is one of the hottest photographers in the biz right now."

"Yes!" Laura said, high-fiving Lara Without.

"Fabulous!" Mindy said. "I love getting all dressed up."

"Are we all doing the shoot?" I asked.

Iris laughed. "Not even close. *Hipster Chick* only picked a handful of girls to do this spread—five in total. And you guys made the cut. So, bravo."

"That's awesome," I said. And I meant it.

"Thank y'all for having faith in me," Mindy said. She was positively glowing. "I promise I'll do ya proud."

"I'm sure you will," Iris said. She talked for a few more minutes, and then was on her way to go meet with some of the other girls.

After Iris had left, Mindy and I settled into our new room (which was cramped, but had an awesome view from the window of Central Park) and mulled over our good fortune.

"Can you believe we're doing the first big assignment?" Mindy asked. "Talk about luck!"

I laughed. "Nah, it's not luck. You heard Iris. They hand-picked us!"

"I wonder who else is going along?"

"I don't know," I said, settling back on my bed. "I guess we'll find out soon enough."

We talked for a little while, getting to know each other a little better. Mindy was friendly, but we were both guarded. The situation was still so fresh, so new, that neither of us was willing to open up and tell all just yet. It was a strange, surreal experience.

Mindy March was not the kind of girl I'd ever be friends with in the real world. But in the fake, bizarre existence that had been created for us by Vamp Modeling, I loved her.

We had little in common. She was a pop-culture aficionado, who knew all the latest tabloid gossip, not to mention the sordid he-said/she-said details of the latest Paris Hilton and Nicole Richie and Lindsay Lohan and Jessica Simpson catfights. (I couldn't keep any of it straight. It seemed like every other day the heiress was dueling with someone new.)

Mindy had never read a book in her entire life. ("Except the ones they, like, make us read for school—but even then I usually just go CliffsNotes," she'd informed me.) And, in keeping with the tradition, Mindy was a size two. As far as I could tell, I was the only plus-sized girl who'd won a spot in the contest.

Which suited me just fine. It guaranteed that, no matter what, I would stand out from the pack.

THREE

How we'd managed to slip into town without being noticed I'll never know. Apparently the other model search winners were getting mobbed right from the moment they arrived at the airport. Vamp Modeling and *Hipster Chick* had done an excellent job of getting the word out about "the hot new crop of models, poised and ready to take the fashion world by storm!"

But for Mindy and I, the mobbing didn't start until the next day.

We were up, bright and early, getting ready to head out on our go see's. We were beyond excited, yet neither of us could have predicted how the day would turn out.

"Make sure you look good, but don't go overboard,"

Mindy informed me, as she applied a light coat of lip gloss. "You don't want to get totally done up for go see's. The clients want you to be a blank canvas. They want to be able to make you into whatever they need you to be."

"Uh-huh," I said, grateful for the advice.

Ever since Iris scolded me the previous day, I'd been studying up on the modeling world. I'd been poring over magazines and doing my best to soak up advice and tips from the other girls. I'd gotten up extra early this morning (around four A.M.) and spent a few hours online reading up about Vamp Modeling, *Hipster Chick,* and the industry as a whole. (I also spent a little time checking out the endless supply of Dex Holcombe fansites. A quick Google search produced thousands of links.)

In truth these are things I should have done sooner. The minute I found out I'd made the cut, I should have been learning all I could about the fashion industry.

In my "real life" I always took things seriously. Whether it was helping solve a friend's boyfriend crisis or finishing out the prep course for my SATs, I made sure I gave it one hundred and ten percent. Yet I'd been treating this modeling thing like a joke. I hadn't done my homework, hadn't arrived in New York prepared. And, from this point forward, that was going to change. I would stop being so wishy-washy, stop having the attitude of *I did this modeling thing on a dare, so what does it matter if I succeed or fail?* And I would start appreciating this for the awesome opportunity that it was. There were, literally, hundreds of thousands of girls who'd tried out. I was one of the few lucky ones. If I squandered my spot, I'd never forgive my-self.

The car service was scheduled to pick Mindy and me up at 6:45 A.M. sharp.

"I don't understand the point of dragging us out of bed at the butt crack of dawn," Mindy complained, as we rode the elevator down to the lobby. "Whatever happened to be-ing fashionably late? As far as I can tell, everyone in this town is all about being early!"

"I feel sorry for the girls like Laura Balcombie who flew in from the West Coast," I said. "Her internal clock is so screwed up. She's used to Pacific time, which is three hours earlier."

"I just hope these go see's aren't too demanding," she said. "I have zero energy."

"Me, too," I said. I was sort of lying. In truth I was wide awake and ready to hit the town. I couldn't wait to get out there and meet the designers and photographers who were going to make us stars.

"I need a coffee," Mindy mumbled, as the elevator doors opened and we stepped out into the lobby. "Do you think they'll let us swing by Dean & Deluca on the way?"

I was so busy marveling over the fact that Dean & De-luca was a real place (we didn't have them in Millew, Ohio, and as far as I'd known it was the fictional coffeehouse where Keri Russell worked on *Felicity*) that I almost missed the swarm of cameramen waiting outside the door to our apartment.

Almost.

"What do ya think they're doing here?" Mindy asked. Suddenly her eyes grew wide. "Do you think someone famous lives here? Maybe Ashlee Simpson? Or Kristin Cavallari?"

"I think they might be . . ." I said, letting my voice trail off. I was going to say, *I think they might be here for us,* but I'd lost my nerve. I'd heard some interesting tales from a few of the other girls while we were unpacking. Liv, a bookwormish beauty, had shared her story of being swarmed as soon as she arrived at the airport. But since Laura B., Lara Without, and I had all made it to our apartment building relatively unnoticed, I'd kind of gotten complacent. I wasn't expecting this.

I mean, honestly. What small-town girl expects the paparazzi to be waiting outside for you at 6:45 in the morning?

The second we got outside the flashbulbs started going off in our faces. I felt like I was moving in slow motion; the ten feet of sidewalk between the door and the car seemed to stretch on forever.

"Look alive!" the driver said, as he held the door to the black Lincoln Town Car open for us.

Mindy climbed in first and I was right behind her.

"Veronika!" I heard all of the photographers shouting my name. "Over here, Veronika! Give us a smile!"

I held my hand up and offered a quick, flirty wave. Then I quickly got into the car.

"That was insane!" Mindy said.

I struggled to catch my breath. I wasn't winded from overexertion; it was nerves. I felt weak in the knees, dizzy with excitement.

All eyes on me. Everybody calling my name. One blinding flashbulb after another, as dozens of cameras captured my every move.

It was the craziest thing I had ever experienced. And also the best.

So *this* was what it felt like to be famous.

THE PAPARAZZI AMBUSH WAS A HARD ACT TO follow. I know "real" celebrities—your Johnny Depps, your Julia Roberts, your Reese Witherspoons—get annoyed by the paparazzi. And I certainly can't blame them. It must be hard to live your life in the spotlight 24/7. But for me the media attention was still so new, so fresh that I couldn't help but eat up every second of it.

And in comparison, the go see's were something of a letdown.

Then again, the fact that I kept getting rejected might have had something to do with it. Over the next five hours, I heard a variety of reasons as to why I wasn't good enough for this designer's collection or that photographer's book.

"You have a great look, but I'm afraid I don't have much use for plus girls at the moment."

"If you'd consider losing forty pounds by next month, we could probably get you in the fall line."

"Your look is pedestrian."

"Our collection is about elegance, and you're a bit too full around the edges."

"Your body isn't refined enough for our clothes."

And on and on it went. They all had pleasant (and not so pleasant) ways of disguising what they really meant. I was too fat to be hired. While Mindy booked job after job, I got turned down over and over again. By midafternoon I was feeling totally deflated.

"I wonder if I'll get sent home early," I said, as Mindy and I grabbed lunch at The Spotted Pig in the West Village.

"Don't be so down on yourself," she said, taking a bite of her fennel and celery salad.

I'd ordered a plate of ham and cooked vegetables—excuse me, prosciutto with roasted radishes—although I didn't much feel like eating. "Maybe if I lose some weight like that one designer recommended . . ."

Mindy shook her head. "There's nothing wrong with being plus-sized." That was easy for her to say. She'd booked four gigs today.

"Wanna trade bodies," I joked.

"Come on, Veronika. Vamp wouldn't have signed you if

they didn't think you had an awesome shot at getting work. You're just hitting a slow patch. Thing's will pick up."

"Maybe," I said, still not convinced.

Mindy speared a hunk of celery with her fork. "It's your first day. Tomorrow will be better, you'll see."

I picked at my ham, scooting it around on my plate.

"Besides you've already got one gig lined up," Mindy pointed out. "We're doing the *Hipster Chick* shoot tomorrow morning! Out of all the girls here, you were one of the only ones picked for that job."

I perked up. "That's true. It should be really awesome."

"And then tomorrow night we've got that party with Dex Holcombe."

I nearly knocked over my glass of mineral water. "What did you just say?"

"We've got a party tomorrow with Dex Holcombe."

"You're joking, right?"

She shook her head. "I heard Laura Balcombie talking about it while I was drying my hair this morning. We're going to hit the clubs tomorrow around nine o'clock, and then afterward the agency has arranged a small party in honor of Dex. We've all been invited."

Oh. My. God. A party with Dex Holcombe? It seemed too good to be true. "What time does the party start?"

"Around midnight, I think," Mindy said. "But I'm not sure. We'll have to get all the details from Iris later. What are you going to wear? I was thinking I'd go with this awesome top I got at Bergdorf's. It's red and . . ."

She kept talking, but I tuned her out. I couldn't help it. All I could think about was the party tomorrow night. And Dex Holcombe.

FOUR

THE DRESS WAS SHEER, BLACK, AND FOUR SIZES too small.

"They told me a plus girl was coming," the wardrobe stylist complained the next morning as he fitted us for the *Hipster Chick* shoot. "I don't understand what the problem is; I brought her an *eight*."

"She needs a twelve," Iris said.

"Twelve!" From the way he said it, you'd have thought Iris had requested he bring me a thirty-eight.

"Twelve," Iris confirmed.

He *tsk-tsk*ed me. "I didn't know we were hosting the fat farm today."

Jesus.

"*Hipster Chick* wants this issue to feature hot winter formal dresses for various types of girls," Iris informed him.

"And whales," the assistant mumbled under his breath.

I'd had about enough of his attitude. "Sure thing, baldie," I said, raising my eyebrows at his receding hairline.

"Bitchy fat women," he said, stalking off.

"Don't mind him," Iris told me, tousling my hair. "He thinks everyone's fat. Laura Balcombie came in earlier today for a fitting, and Joe Sherpa couldn't stop moaning about what a heifer she was."

Joe Sherpa. So that was the evil wardrobe stylist's name. It was pretty insane, if you thought about it. Laura B. was frighteningly thin, the kind of girl who would be swimming in a size zero. I think she told me she wore a negative two.

A few minutes later he was back with a size ten gown. "I highly doubt this thing will zip up, but we can hold it together in the back with some swaths of material and a few pins."

"Joe!" Iris said. "You know this is an action shot. The dress'll never stay put."

"Not my problem."

"It's going to be if we don't get a good photo."

"Sorry, this is the best I can do," he offered, sounding less than enthused to be working with me.

"It'll be all right," I said. "I'm sure I can pose so the dress stays on."

"I hope so," Iris said, as Joe began pulling the dress around me. "Otherwise, we're going to wind up with a bunch of triple X shots."

A few minutes later my hair and makeup had been touched up and I was getting ready to start my very first photo shoot for Vamp Modeling. It was going to be glamorous, it was going to be magical, it was going to be . . .

On a mechanical bull.

Yep, that's right. *Hipster Chick* and Vamp Modeling wanted me to straddle a mechanical bull in a skintight strapless evening gown with Marc Jacobs heels and an elegant upsweep.

"This is Trudie, your photographer," Iris said, introducing us.

We shook hands and exchanged pleasantries. Then Trudie got right to work instructing me on how the shoot would go.

"Do you have any tips?" I asked.

"Only about a million." Trudie laughed. "I know this is a little wacky, but I want you to try and relax and not worry about the mechanical bull. We're going to leave it on the lowest setting," Trudie informed me, crouching down on the floor, camera in hand. "Just have fun with it. Throw your arms up in the air. Laugh. Smile. Be sexy. Coy." She ticked off a list of different facial expressions and moods. "The best pictures are when you act natural and have fun, but also remember to always keep your focus on the camera."

When she had finished explaining, I made my way over to the bull and, as gracefully as possible, climbed on top. Unfortunately I also managed to nearly lose the top of my dress in the process.

"Oops!" I said, rushing to cover my chest. "Didn't mean to flash you guys."

Joe snickered.

I hoisted the top of my dress up over my partially exposed cleavage. Once I was covered up again, the shoot officially started.

"Go! Start it! Go!" I heard Trudie call out. Someone hit a switch and the bull came to life, rocking me back and forth as it turned me in slow circles.

"Come on, honey, work it!" Iris called out. "Show us your sex appeal!"

I struck my sexiest pose, leaning forward and spreading my mouth into a sweet, yet naughty, smile. I was doing a great job, if I did say so myself. Unfortunately I was the only one who thought so.

"Cut!" Trudie yelled. "You're giving me nothing." She massaged her temples. "Talk to her," she said, walking off.

Iris came over. "Veronika, baby, you're going to have to try a little harder. When we met you in Ohio last May you were fierce. Right now you're dull. Lifeless. Boring as a lump of wet paper."

I grimaced at the unexpected insult. "Okay, I'll try something different."

"I need you to loosen up, while simultaneously becoming more intense, more focused."

Okaaaaaaaay.

"Are we clear?"

Not really. "Yep, crystal." I got back in the saddle. Literally.

"Give me something fierce! Flirty! Fun!" Trudie instructed.

I quickly struck a few poses. Then I felt a yawn coming on and I fought hard to suppress it. No such luck. Next thing I knew, my mouth had popped open really wide, and the yawn came out. I couldn't help it. I was exhausted. I was afraid Trudie would mistake it for boredom, but she ate it up.

"That's it! Show me your fangs!"

Iris made a quick "kill" motion—slicing her finger across her neck, and Trudie blushed.

"Show me your teeth!" she said.

I opened my mouth again, giving her a coy, sassy—and slightly vicious—grin.

I must have been doing something right, because Trudie got really excited. "That's it, Veronika!" she said, snapping away furiously with her camera. "Less pretty girl, more vixen. More"—she paused dramatically—"vamp."

* * *

"Have you ever danced on a table before?"
the bartender asked Mindy. It was just past nine thirty, and
we were downing cosmos and oyster cocktails in the VIP
lounge at Apocalypse, a trendy club.

"No," she said, shouting to be heard over the *thump
thump thump* of the bass line. The DJ was playing a mix-
ture of techno and rap. In a few minutes, a hot new recording artist named Jackson Lowe was scheduled to take the
stage and treat us to a live performance of his upcoming
CD. He was one of the most buzzed about new artists and
getting a pass to this show was next to impossible. The tables were filled with a veritable who's who of the New York
club scene. Everyone from Paris Hilton to Brandon Davis to
Jessica Simpson was here to catch the show. And amazingly
the models of Vamp had been invited.

Convinced that Mindy was a lost cause, the bartender
turned to me. "What about you?" he asked, pouring me
another drink. "You look like the kind of girl who likes to
have fun."

It was a really bad, obvious line. And he was staring at
my chest, although I couldn't exactly blame him. Vamp had
given me several complimentary dresses and tops, including
the one I was currently wearing. The clothes were not only
gorgeous and expensive—they were also incredibly revealing. My breasts were hiked up so high they looked Isaac-

Mizrahi-grabs-Scarlett-Johansson's-boobs-at-the-Golden-Globes gargantuan.

"I'm all about fun," I said, in answer to his question.

He patted the bar top. "Then get your butt up here." He had clearly lost his mind. No way in hell I was getting on top of the bar.

"No thanks." I sipped my drink.

"Come on!" he pleaded. "I'll play you a song. Anything you like."

"Well . . ." I toyed with him while I thought it over. It was tempting. I was hundreds of miles away from home. No one here *really* knew me.

"You should go for it," a deep voice said right beside me. Dex Holcombe moved in, placing his hand on my arm. I felt the hairs on the back of my neck stand up. "I can't imagine anything sexier than seeing you up there, shaking your stuff."

I know it's wrong to do something because a guy encourages you to. I know it's stupid to get caught up in the moment and act irrationally just to impress someone you have a crush on. But right at that moment, I didn't care.

As Dex watched, I hoisted myself up onto the bar counter and stood up, shakily in my Manolos.

"Veronika . . ." Mindy said, chewing nervously on her lip.

"Hell yes!" the bartender said. "This is more like it."

I stood there, awkwardly for a minute, not sure of what to do. Suddenly Dex jumped up beside me. "Come on, V," he said, inventing a new spur-of-the-moment nickname for me. "Let's show 'em how it's done."

Next thing I knew we were dancing and swaying, bumping and grinding, as a 50 Cent song blared in the background. Dex pulled me against him. We stayed up there for two songs before jumping down. After that the night went by in a blur of drinks and dancing, while Jackson Lowe played set after awesome set in the background. The guy was majorly talented. I could see why he'd gotten a huge recording contract before his eighteenth birthday.

"I have to leave," Dex told me around midnight. "I'll see you at the after party, right?" he asked.

I nodded, woozy from the alcohol and from being so close to him. "Definitely. I can't wait."

And then he was gone. I stood there, feeling alone and despondent. I couldn't find Mindy anywhere. In fact none of the Vamp girls were around. I felt panicked, unsure of what to do next.

"That was quite a show," someone said. I turned around to find Jackson Lowe standing next to me.

"You were awesome!" I said, giving him an enthusiastic high five. "Freaky-deaky, out of this world, effing awesome!" I was too drunk to realize how weird I was acting.

Jackson cocked his head. "Thanks. I was talking about you, though. I enjoyed your little dance routine earlier tonight."

I blushed. "Oh, *that*."

"Who was that guy? Your boyfriend?"

Oh my God. Was this going where I thought?

"No, he's a . . . coworker," I said, finally settling on a way to put it. It might not have been one hundred percent truthful—after the way he'd been dancing with me, I suspected Dex and I were going to become more than just colleagues pretty soon—but it had grains of truth.

"Good. I was thinking we could go out sometime."

I laughed, surprised. "Are you always this forward?"

Jackson smiled. "No. But I like you. And I'm smart enough to act quickly. New York minute and all that," he said.

"I see." I paused, and we stared at each other for a minute. "I'm Veronika, by the way."

"I know. I asked your friend Mindy. You work with Vamp Modeling Inc., don't you?"

I nodded. "Here, give me your hand." I took out a pen and scrawled my digits across his palm. I was so out of it that I accidentally wrote down my parents' number in Ohio. "Oh, wait!" I said, catching my mistake. "Let me give you my current number." I tried frantically to blot out my home digits. The last thing I needed was for him to ring up my folks back in Mildew. "Here, this is where you can reach me in New York," I said, writing down the correct number.

"Great, thanks, Veronika," he said. "I'll give you a call

tomorrow." And then, quickly and confidently, Jackson Lowe leaned in and kissed me on the cheek. "Talk to you soon."

Without a doubt, this had to be the craziest night of my entire life.

In the span of a few short hours, I had gone from having no prospects to having two incredibly hot, incredibly famous guys ask me out.

Viva New York!

FIVE

I RODE OVER TO THE PARTY WITH MINDY, LAURA B., and Olivia, a.k.a. Liv. We got there just past twelve thirty. I was surprised to find Dex Holcombe waiting for me at the door.

"I'm so glad you're here," he said, grabbing my hand and leading me into the room. "The party's just getting started."

It was funny, because back home the party would have been already over three hours ago. Teens in Mildew rarely stayed out past nine or ten at night. It wasn't because our parents were strict. There was simply nothing to do. We didn't have a movie theater or a shopping mall or any underage clubs. Come to think of it, we didn't have any *over*age clubs, either. But at least if you were twenty-one you could go out drinking in one of Mildew's four bars. The rest of us were totally screwed.

"Here, I got you a drink," Dex said, handing me something that looked like a martini and tasted like Clorox. (Not that I've ever swigged a mouthful of bleach. But you know what I mean.) "It's a vodka gimlet," he said. Then he led me out into the center of the living room, which was serving as a de facto dance floor.

Four drinks and a dozen slow dances later, we wound up on the balcony, huddled close despite the scorching June heat.

"I *love* being with you."

I had a brief, stupid, girlie moment where I thought he was going to say he loved me. I have to admit I was a little relieved that he didn't.

Dex started rambling. "I think it's awesome to find a girl who's so confident about her body. Most of the chicks I've dated have been toothpicks. I touch them and I feel like they'll break. Not you, though. You're a real woman."

I wasn't sure whether to take this as a compliment or an insult. He'd basically just called me chubby, but in the context it suddenly didn't sound like such a bad thing. I squeezed his hand. "Thanks."

It was weird how, after being with him for a while, I kind of forgot who he was. The shock of it began to wear off. Instead of focusing on thoughts of *Oh my God I'm here with the world famous Dex Holcombe!* I just relaxed and let myself get swept up in the moment.

Which is probably why I let it happen.

"Let's go," Dex said, "somewhere we can be alone." He steered me out onto the balcony and I didn't resist. "God, you look great tonight," he said, stroking my face with his fingers. He pushed a lock of my red hair off my cheek.

"Thanks," I said. I felt dizzy, and my body tingled. I couldn't tell if it was from the drinks or his touch. I decided on the latter.

Dex leaned forward, until our faces were practically touching. "I thought I'd never get you alone," he whispered. I could feel his breath tickling my ear and it made me giddy.

Before I could say anything it happened. Suddenly, almost instinctively, we moved our mouths together.

I felt Dex's lips on mine. He kissed the corners of my mouth, tenderly, softly, and then moved on to my chin. He traced his mouth over my face—kissing my lips, my chin, my neck.

As he moved along, concentrating his efforts on my neck, I felt myself growing woozy. The four vodka gimlets I'd downed were starting to take their toll. Add to that the fact that I'd skipped dinner. . . .

Suddenly he started to get rough. His teeth scraped against my neck, hard and sharp and painful.

"Ow," I said, trying to push him away.

He kept going. He kept getting rougher.

And then he drew blood. I felt it, warm and wet against my neck. He ran his tongue along, lapping it up.

"Dex, stop," I mumbled, feeling powerless to do anything.

"You'll love this, I swear," he said, holding me tightly. "What I'm doing . . . how I'm changing you. It's going to feel so good!"

Holy shit! The way he was talking . . . Was he planning to devirginize me? I figured he couldn't be. After all Dex had no way of even knowing I was a member of the V club. It wasn't like I'd advertised it.

"You're not gonna," I began. "I don't wanna . . . do anything weird. I don't want to . . ." I struggled to get the words out. "Sleep with you," I finally said. I felt like I was going to hurl.

"Don't be crazy," Dex told me, as he kissed the side of my face. "I just tasted your blood. Now it's your turn."

"Wh-what?!"

"Kiss my neck," he instructed me, pulling my face against his. "And don't stop until you taste blood."

Everything after that went by in a blur. I remember more dancing, kissing. I remember Dex holding me. I remember the other girls—Mindy, Laura B., the bookwormish Liv—moving in and out of the party. I know I talked to some of them, but I can't even recall what I said.

And I remember the blood. My blood, his. I have no idea where it came from, how it happened.

Or how it ended.

One moment I was there, the next I was gone. I just disappeared, faded away, in a haze of vodka and Dex. Sometime, while his lips moved lower, tracing patterns on my neck, tasting my blood again, I passed out.

I AWOKE TO THE WORST HANGOVER OF MY LIFE. It was also the *first* hangover of my life. Even with all of my clubbing and partying and dancing on bar tops and downing cosmos I had never experienced anything like this.

I was nauseous, but my body felt sluggish and heavy, as though I'd been weighted down under a thousand pounds. I tried to pull myself out of bed. I knew I'd feel better if I had something to eat and quenched my dehydrated body. But the thought of eating or drinking anything made my stomach lurch.

I tried, in vain, to fall back asleep. I could hear someone moaning across the room.

"Oooohhhhmmmmmm."

I tried to ignore her, but the moans got louder. A burst of undetectable words and noises.

"Hhhhhalllmmeeeee."

"Mindy?" I mumbled.

"Heeeelllllp."

I was finally able to decipher it. *Help.* Yikes. That finally got me out of bed. "Are you okay?" I asked, staggering across the room.

Mindy was lumped in a pile in the corner. She looked pale, sickly. I leaned down, trying to help her up. She tipped forward, gagging. Thankfully she didn't throw up. I helped her back to bed, and then got her a cup of ginger ale from the kitchen. My knees felt wobbly and my body ached, but Mindy was in such terrible shape that it took my mind off my own problems.

"Something happened at that party last night," I heard someone say.

I whirled around. Laura Balcombie was standing in the doorway to our room.

"What do you mean?" I asked.

"Lara's sick, too. Most of the girls are."

I felt chilled. "But that doesn't make sense. With Mindy and me it could be the vodka gimlets. But Lara doesn't even drink. . . ."

"It must be food poisoning."

"We're models," I said. "None of us ate." There was some definite truth to the myths. It wasn't that models never ate. But, well, we didn't eat much. Or often. Even me, a proud size twelve, had been dodging meals since I'd arrived at Vamp.

"I think Lara needs a doctor," she said nervously.

"Mindy, too."

We looked at each other, neither of us sure what to do.

"I'll call Iris," I said finally, grabbing the phone. I frantically dialed her number. I was afraid it would go through to voice mail, but she answered on the first ring. "Iris!" I screamed.

"Is this Veronika?" she asked, obviously unfazed by my panicked tone.

"Yes. Everybody's sick! We need a doctor. Should I call the car service and go to the hospital or can you guys bring someone here?"

Iris laughed. "You're not sick."

"But Mindy and Lara—"

"Trust me. They'll be fine."

"Iris," I said, my voice breaking. I was on the verge of tears. This, from the girl who never cries at anything. "I'm really worried. I don't think you realize how bad they are."

"I'm on my way over," she said. "I'll be there in ten minutes."

"With a doctor?" I prompted.

"I'm bringing help, yes," Iris assured me.

I breathed a sigh of relief. "Thanks."

"I understand why you're upset," Iris said. "But as soon as I get there you'll feel much better. All of you."

I wasn't so sure of that, but I didn't argue.

"I have just the thing to take care of what's ailing you."

"Medicine?" I asked.

"Yes. Sort of."

Sort of? "You're not bringing, uh, pharms are you?"

Pharms was the code word for Rx pills with a kick. You know, Valium, Oxy, anything you can crush up or snort or use recreationally. Or, at least, that's what I'd heard. Thus far, none of the Vamp model search winners were dabbling in the drug pool. But given Iris's coke comment on day one, you could never be too sure.

"No, nothing like that. I'm bringing some food," she said.

"Food?"

"Yes, food. Once the girls eat—and once they get the, *ahem*, treatment they need, everything will be fine."

I wanted to trust her, but something told me not to.

BY THE TIME IRIS FINALLY ARRIVED MINDY HAD thrown up twice and Lara Without had nearly fainted. Laura and I paced the apartment nervously while we waited. When Iris finally showed up—a full half hour later than she'd said—we were sick with fear.

"Hi, girls," she said, giving us air kisses as she came in the door. She looked flushed and happy, excited to be here. "I've got just the thing to make you feel better," she said, stepping aside to reveal the big surprise.

Dex Holcombe came strolling in, carrying a tray of coffee cups from Starbucks.

Coffee? This was the magic recipe to make us well again? Was Iris joking?

"Hey," Dex said flatly. He walked over to the couch and flopped down.

I stared at him in shock. What was he doing here? It didn't make sense. Ordinarily I would have been horrified to have a hot guy—especially one I'd just made out with the night before—see me in this state. My hair was matted, I was dressed in my ugliest pajamas, and I still had sleep crust caked around my eyes.

No matter—Mindy and Lara Without had to come first. At the moment, Dex was the last thing I was worried about.

Although, in retrospect, he should have been the first.

"I turned you," he told me proudly. "All of you."

"What?"

"I turned you last night!"

"What are you talking about?" Laura B. asked. "What did you turn us . . . gay?"

"You're getting ahead of yourself," Iris told him. "And, technically, you didn't turn them *all*. Just Veronika and Lara, right?"

"I spiked the drinks, though," he said.

Now I was getting angry. "What do you mean you spiked our drinks!?" I demanded.

"I slipped you something."

"Dex—" Iris warned.

"Nothing harmful. Just a little something to get you in the mood. And it worked, too."

Get us in the mood? "My God, what did you do, rape us?"

He laughed. "Not even close. Like I said before, I *turned* you."

This was infuriating. *He* was infuriating. I couldn't believe I'd ever wasted one second liking a guy like Dex Holcombe. He was obviously nothing more than a drink-spiking, underage-girl-taking-advantage-of jackass.

"Girls," Iris said. She picked up the coffee tray. "Drink this. It will make you feel better."

"I'm not drinking anything you people give me," Laura B. said indignantly.

I had to agree. "Ditto."

"Drink it," Iris said, looking cross. "You'll feel better; I can guarantee that."

Did she think we were crazy? "Dex comes in here and admits to spiking our drinks last night and now you expect us to just randomly accept more stuff from him? Are you nuts?"

Before Iris could respond, Mindy—who'd been lying there like a zombie this entire time—suddenly sprang to life. She reached over and snatched one of the coffee cups from the tray, downing the liquid in one go.

"What the he—?" she asked.

"Did you like it?" Iris asked, winking at her.

"That wasn't . . . well, it wasn't." She stopped, confused.

"No, it wasn't," Iris said cryptically. "But what about the taste? Delicious, huh?" she asked.

Dex smiled knowingly. "Best you've ever had, I bet."

Mindy closed her eyes and sighed. "Yes. I've never in my life felt anything like that. It was sooooo good!"

I stared at her. "You're acting like you've never had coffee before."

"It's not coffee," Mindy said. All at once she looked bright eyed and energetic, back to her old self.

"What is it then?" I asked, addressing my question to Iris. "This miracle potion you're saying will make us better?"

"Blood," Iris said simply.

"Blood?" Laura B. sputtered.

I expected Mindy to freak out and start gagging. But she didn't. Instead she asked for another cup.

"Those are for the rest of the girls," Iris said, moving the tray out of her reach. "Your whole apartment was turned last night and we've got to make sure they all get their nourishment."

"That's why you all feel so sick," Dex said. "You're horribly malnourished. You need to get some fluids in you right away."

"Some fluids . . . like blood?" I asked. "Is this an elaborate practical joke? Are you guys just setting us up to look stupid?"

Dex shook his head. "Not at all. This is who you are now. You're one of us."

"One of you?" I repeated. My skull was throbbing. It was all too much to process. Any minute I expected to wake up and find myself back home in Mildew, this whole experience a weird, lucid dream.

"You're a vamp," Iris said quietly.

"A vamp? As in a sexy vampish model?" Laura B. asked.

"No," Iris said. "As in a vampire."

SIX

MINDY BURST INTO TEARS.

"This isn't very funny," Laura B. said.

"You tricked us!" Mindy seconded.

I just sat there, unable to say anything.

"It may seem strange now, but you'll thank us later," Dex said. "I know when I first got changed I was livid. But once I sat back and realized all of the benefits to being a vampire . . . Well, I now see that it's the best thing that could have happened to me."

Iris nodded. "You're a member of the elite. You'll never grow old. You'll be young and fresh and beautiful forever."

It reminded me of that Oscar Wilde book, *The Picture*

of Dorian Gray. The one where the guy loses his mind trying to find eternal youth.

Iris began explaining. "We've done this for two reasons. One, you can stay young and perfect looking forever. Which means you can work in the fashion industry forever, earning scads of money along the way."

"And, two," Dex said, taking over where she'd left off. "It keeps the vampire race exclusively good looking. And there's nothing sexier, nothing hotter, than a drop-dead gorgeous legion of vampires."

I was dangerously close to puking.

"In order to turn someone into a bloodsucker, you've got to first obtain permission from the Vampires' League. Which is why they love working with us so much," Iris explained. "We bring them the finest specimens of vampires."

"This is a very selective group you now belong to," Dex finished. "You should be proud. The League doesn't just allow any Joe Blow Average to walk in off the street and become a vamp. You have to really stand out to be accepted. Consider yourselves lucky."

Somehow I didn't feel lucky. I felt nauseous.

It all made so much sense now. I felt like the dumbest person on the face of planet earth.

"But wait a minute . . . How are you going to take our pictures?" Laura B. asked smugly. "Vampires don't show up on film."

Dex rolled his eyes. "Of all the myths out there, that one pisses me off the most. It's stupid and illogical. If you can see vampires with the human eye—and we all know you can—then a camera can capture them."

"It's basic physics," Iris said. "Vampires show up on photographs because they're solid objects and they reflect light, which is how photography works in the first place. Light bounces off an object and is captured by the camera. Hence the reason you can't take photos in the dark."

"This science lesson is grating on my last nerve," Laura B. complained, looking outraged. "I don't care if vampires can show up on film or whatever the hell the truth really is. I don't want to be one! You had no right to do this to me! I can sue you." She paused, laughing wickedly. "I *will* sue you."

"Go ahead," Iris said, looking unconcerned. "Just remember, you'll be angering a very powerful group of people. Some of the most famous, most successful members of society are vamps. You don't want to wind up their enemy."

Dex chuckled. "That's assuming you could get a lawyer to take your case in the first place. They'd laugh you right out of the courtroom." He wagged his finger in her direction. "And if you alienate yourself from the vampire clan like that, you'll be sorry. Take my word for it."

"I know this is a difficult adjustment," Iris said. "But once you've had some time to get used to the idea, once you've settled in, I think you'll find you really love your new life."

"And if we don't?" Mindy asked.

Iris didn't answer. Instead she and Dex stood up and prepared to go.

"One more thing," she said, as she made her way to the door. "From here on out, you can't have *any* food. You understand? Your body will respond to it like poison. It's blood, blood, and more blood from this point out."

"What about drinks?" Mindy asked, squeezing a fresh set of tears out of her eyes. "Can we still have vodka and stuff like that?"

"'Fraid not," Dex said. "But you won't miss it." He grinned. "Trust me. Once you get accustomed to the blood, you're going to love it. There's so many awesome varieties. A positive and AB negative are my two favorites. Unfortunately they're harder to come by. But O positive, which is what you guys are drinking"—he gestured toward the coffee tray—"is still really good stuff. Very satisfying." He made a face. "But a little advice. Stay away from O neg. It's vile."

What was he, the vampire gourmet?

"Try to get some rest," Iris said. "Oh, and don't forget to drink up. You'll feel so much better once you do. I'll have another shipment brought over later on tonight. So enjoy!"

And with that, they were gone.

The second they'd left, Mindy and Laura B. both burst into tears.

I ignored them and turned to face the mirror and discovered that, much to my surprise, my reflection was showing. I wrinkled my brow. I thought vampires didn't have reflections. I suppose that could have been another myth, like the photography.

Or else . . .

What if this was just an elaborate practical joke? What if Iris and company had decided to mess with our heads, to see how far they could take it before we wised up and realized they were playing us? It would only make sense. There was no way we could really be vampires. Vampires didn't even exist. Iris and Dex were jerking our chains.

And, I have to admit, I felt strangely disappointed when I realized this. It wasn't that I wanted to be a vampire per se. But, well, there had been something intriguing about all of it. The immortality part. The exclusive club. The idea of being in on this huge, worldly secret. And it was all a sham.

Those assholes!

The longer I thought about it, the angrier I got. What right did they have to jerk us around like this? To play mean, elaborate practical jokes on their star models. I ought to sue them for providing false information. At the very least, I would give Iris D'Abruzzo a piece of my mind.

I was practically foaming at the mouth. And then, as I turned to go, I caught sight of myself in the mirror once again. My mouth was open slightly and there, protruding from my gums, were a set of sharp, vicious-looking fangs.

Somebody—Mindy, I think—let out a bloodcurdling scream.

I should have been scared. I should have been nauseous and upset. But all I could do was smile.

"Cool!" I whispered under my breath, as I spread my lips apart, revealing a new-and-improved smile. Then I picked up one of the blood-filled coffee cups, tipped my head back, and gulped it down in one go.

SEVEN

I'VE GIVEN THIS SOME THOUGHT.

There are definite advantages to being a vampire. Most of the other girls—Laura B. and Mindy, included—don't see it this way.

They're devastated. Horrified. They don't like the idea of being unknowingly (and unwillingly) brought over to the dark side.

Personally I couldn't be happier. It might sound crazy. It might sound strange. But I'm telling you. This vamp thing is beyond awesome. Without further adieu, I give you:

Veronika James's Top Ten Reasons Being a Vampire Rocks

1. I will never, ever have to worry about wrinkles, saggy boobs, or any of those other annoying "old lady" troubles. This is great news. My mother has not aged particularly well. At forty-eight, she is covered with crow's feet and sunspots and all sorts of nasty age-related problems. I will be able to sidestep all of these. No expensive wrinkle-reducing creams. No scary Botox shots. I will age (or not, as the case may be) with grace and style.

2. Fangs. Not to be creepy, but fangs are hot.

3. I can party all night long without getting bags under my eyes.

4. I get to be fearless. All the things mortals fret over—gun crime, disease, death—can't touch me anymore. In a way, I'm invincible.

5. Unless someone decides to stake me. But what are the odds of that happening?

6. I'm part of an exclusive club. According to Iris D'Abruzzo, only the hottest people are "turned." It's how they keep the vampire group sexy, young, and desirable.

7. I'm in some damn fine company. Bloodsuckers are sexy. Look at Dex Holcombe. Or Brad Pitt in that *Interview with the Vampire* movie. Or Spike from *Buffy the Vampire Slayer*.

8. If some überbitch, a la Kerry Malone, every screws with me again I can take a bite of her—literally.

9. I get to be a myth, a legend.

10. I will be seventeen forever. Have I mentioned how cool this is?!?!

I thought I had it all ironed out. But when I showed Mindy my list, she got really mad.

"You obviously haven't thought this through," she said, glaring at me. "So what if we get to live forever? Everyone we know is going to grow up and die, and we'll be left behind."

"Not necessarily," I said. "We could turn them."

"No we couldn't! Didn't you hear what Iris and Dex said?"

"Yes."

"You can't change anyone without getting permission first," she reminded me.

She was right. "Maybe that won't be so bad."

"Watching our families die won't be bad? Are you honestly that cruel?"

Before I could point out that, no matter what, we'd still have each other, we'd still have our fellow vampires, she cut me off.

"Big deal. Our friends and family aren't going to be vamps. We'll lose them all. We'll never get the chance to grow up. Not properly. We're going to get stuck in this weird, inbetween state for the rest of our lives."

"But what about the list?" I asked, waving it in her face. "Didn't you read it?"

"I read it. And your points are totally dumb," Mindy said, rolling her eyes. "They're shallow. Superficial. The kind of thing Paris Hilton would come up with. I would have expected more from you, Veronika."

I started to defend myself but then the phone rang. "It's for you!" Lara Without called.

I dashed out into the living room and picked up the receiver. "Hello," I said.

"Hi, Veronika. It's Jackson Lowe."

"Jackson!" In all the excitement over the party and the vampire revelation, I'd completely forgotten that Jackson was supposed to call today.

"How are you?" he asked.

What to say? I certainly couldn't tell him the truth. "I'm great."

"You up for getting some food? I know a great Italian place in the Village."

Uh-oh. I couldn't eat anything but blood. . . . Then again

I could always go, claim I was watching my figure, and just order a glass of water. "Sounds like fun," I told him. "When do you want to hook up?"

"How about I pick you up in an hour? Will that give you enough time?"

"Sure," I said, trying to keep my tone casual. I gave him directions to my apartment, and we hung up.

It was funny. Just last night I'd been musing over how both Jackson and Dex liked me. I'd been wondering if I could possibly juggle two different guys at once. Now it seemed ludicrous. I wouldn't touch Dex Holcombe with a ten-foot pole.

I went into the bedroom and told Mindy my good news.

She didn't seem very happy for me.

"Better call back and get him to change the restaurant." She flopped onto the bed, facedown. "You're forgetting. We can't eat garlic."

"We can't eat *anything*," I pointed out. "Except blood."

"Yeah, but being in an Italian restaurant—around all that garlicky food," she said, "I'm not sure it's such a good idea. But suit yourself. If you want to go find out firsthand, I won't stop you."

"Maybe the garlic thing is a myth, like the photographs."

"You can test out that theory and let me know, 'kay?" Mindy said, putting the pillow over her head and going to sleep.

I decided not to chance it. I called Iris's cell and told her my predicament. She was thrilled that I was going out with Jackson Lowe. "Anything to keep you girls in the tabloids," she said. Unfortunately she wasn't so thrilled with Jackson's choice of restaurant. The garlic thing, as it turned out, was not a myth.

"You'd better reschedule. Or else feign a sudden allergy to pasta."

"Yeah, but what restaurant doesn't use garlic in their foods?" I asked. "I mean, if we go to Chinese or Mexican or something, won't I run across the same problem?"

"Not to the degree you will at Italian restaurants. I wouldn't try it, sweetie," Iris cautioned me. "I've seen the reactions vamps get when garlic touches their skin. Even a tiny drop of it will sear your flesh off."

With that lovely image in mind, I called Jackson back. "I was wondering something. I know you said you were in the mood for Italian, but I know a great little coffee shop that serves sandwiches and stuff. I was hoping we could go there instead. You know, that way we could really relax and get to know each other."

Jackson agreed. An hour later we were sitting in the coffee shop. I pretended to sip water, and picked at a blueberry bagel. (Despite my protests, Jackson had insisted I order something. Fortunately he hadn't noticed that I'd been moving it around my plate, not taking any bites.)

"So tell me why you came to New York?" he asked.

I launched into the story of Kerry Malone and the modeling contest dare. He laughed at all the right parts, smiling and listening and encouraging me to say more. It was a total change from the guys back home, most of whom seemed bent on getting up your shirt instead of into your mind.

"That seems like a million years ago," I said. And it really did. It had only been a few days since I'd arrived and it already felt like I'd been here a lifetime. I guess it wasn't weird, considering my entire life—right down to my DNA—was different now.

Jackson told me about his record deal. How he'd been a child prodigy, learning to play guitar before he'd learned to ride a bike. "I did the local touring circuit back home in Bakersfield, California. And on the weekends I'd go into L.A. and try to get gigs doing backup for different musicians."

But his real passion had been writing his own music. Before long he'd started booking his own gigs and playing his own songs. One thing lead to another, and an A&R rep from Interscope fell totally in love with his music. A seven-figure bidding war later, he was in New York, preparing to release his new album in less than two weeks.

"It sounds like such a whirlwind!" I said, excited by the story.

"It has been," he said, looking uncomfortable. "But it's also a lot of pressure. I worry that I'm not going to live up to the hype."

"You will," I assured him. And I really believed it.

"So tell me more about the agency you're with. Vamp Modeling Inc.," Jackson mused. "That's kind of a weird name."

"You think?" I asked nervously. Now that I knew the "big secret," the name seemed like such a dead giveaway.

"Yeah. What are they trying to sell you as? Goth girls?"

I laughed it off. "No. It just means that we vamp it up with style when we're out on assignment. You know, we *bring it*," I said, snapping my fingers.

"Maybe." He shrugged, leaning back in his chair. "It still sounds goth girl to me."

"But there are plenty of guys at the agency," I said.

"Which totally makes no sense," Jackson said, sipping his coffee. "I wouldn't sign with, say, Righteous Babe Records."

I giggled.

"You laugh, but that's a real company. It was founded by Ani DiFranco." Seeing my blank expression, he added, "She's pretty much one of the hottest indie artists of all time. Damn, Veronika, you're so clueless about this stuff, aren't you?"

I chewed on my lower lip. "Kind of. But I'm learning."

"And I'm just the one to teach you," Jackson said, putting his arm around me. "About everything." He looked into my eyes for a long moment, and then leaned across the table and brushed his lips softly against mine.

It would have been an amazingly tender moment if not for the rude interruption. Suddenly the coffee shop was filled with the the loud catcalls, clicks, and flashbulbs of the paparazzi who had gathered outside the door.

"When did they get here?" Jackson asked, looking annoyed.

"Welcome to fame," I said, leaning forward and giving him another kiss.

So what's going on with you and Jackson?" Mindy asked the following day as we got ready to head out on go see's. She looked pale and ghostlike, the result of spending too much time holed up in the apartment. But at least she didn't seem to be mad at me anymore. That was a good sign.

"Nothing, really," I said, trying to be coy.

"C'mon, girl, you can tell me." Mindy pretended to pout. "It's all over Page Six and Defamer. You guys are the hottest item in New York right now."

"We are?" I exclaimed, stunned.

She began pulling up websites on her laptop computer, and one by one, pictures of my first kiss with Jackson popped onto the screen.

"This is insane!"

"Tell me about it," she said.

"My parents are going to freak out!"

"Girl, if I were dating Jackson Lowe my mom would be beyond stoked. How awesome is that? He's such a catch."

"You don't know my parents," I said, feeling panicked. "They freak out about everything. They barely let me come to New York in the first place. Iris spent hours, and I mean *hours*, on the phone with my mom trying to convince her to let me come."

"It's not like they're going to pull the plug and bring you home now," Mindy said.

"They might." This whole thing was surreal. I never imagined it would get this far. I knew the paparazzi had been stalking us, but I'd just figured it was a slow news night without any Paris Hilton catfights to distract them. I hadn't realized Jackson and I had made such a big splash. Besides the pictures they'd snapped of us last weekend had yet to show up anywhere.

At least, as far as I knew.

"With Jackson's album about to drop, the heat must be getting so intense," Mindy said. "His video's debuting on TRL later today so talk about awesome timing!"

It couldn't have been a coincidence. Someone from the record label or, possibly, Vamp must have tipped off the paparazzi.

I felt nervous and shaky all day. It wasn't just the fear of how my parents would react. I was worried about being shadowed this closely by photographers. What if they caught a photo of me in my, um, undead state? What if they captured me lapping up blood or sprouting my giant fangs in all their glory?

My life would be ruined.

EIGHT

Exactly one week later, my worst fear came true.

No, the paparazzi didn't catch me in a vampilicious pose. And no, Jackson didn't turn out to be a snake in the grass, waiting to pounce.

(In fact, he was proving to be quite the sweet and attentive guy. The kind I could fall in love with, under the right circumstances. Not to mention the preorders on his album, *Jump Off a Bridge with Me,* were huge. Every time I saw him, he had some awesome piece of news for me. We were having drinks after I finished talking with Iris.)

No, the fear that came true was worse than any of that.

It was the ultimate fear. The biggest fear that plagues any woman who has ever struggled with her weight.

"I called this meeting with you because we have a little problem on our hands," Iris said.

I knew that by *we,* she really meant *me.*

"I just got your doctor's report in."

I started to panic. What if I was dying? What if the vampire changeover had had a lethal side effect?

"Veronika." Iris sighed. She sounded like my mom. "You've gained thirteen pounds," she said, staring at me across the top of her desk.

"What?! That's impossible!" I exclaimed. "I'm not even eating *food* anymore. If anything, I should have lost weight."

Iris tossed a piece of paper across the desk at me. "The scale doesn't lie."

It was my doctor's printout from my weekly weigh-in. I stared down at the paper in horror. She was right. I'd gained a significant chunk of weight. In less than a week. How was this possible? "I don't understand this *at all*. I'm drinking the same blood as everyone else," I said.

"Are you snacking between meals?" Iris asked.

I burst out laughing. "God, no." What did she think I was doing? Traipsing around Bergdorf's biting random people on the neck and draining their blood? "I don't even have access to more . . . *snacks*."

"You never know." She shrugged. "Look, I don't mean

to alarm you, Veronika. But if you don't get this under control we're going to have no choice but to boot you from the agency."

This was like a bad dream. I knew I'd put on some weight. My clothes were tight, my stomach felt bloated, and my face looked slightly fuller. But why would drinking blood do this to me? And how could I fix it? It wasn't like I could go sign up at Weight Watchers. I'm fairly sure their Points system doesn't accommodate type O positive. And it's not like Lean Cuisine makes low-fat frozen blood meals.

"What do you suggest I do?" I asked, trying to keep my tone even. "I can't go sign up for Jenny Craig. In all her annoying commercials, I never once saw Kirstie Alley mention anything about a special program for vampires."

Iris was not amused. "You can joke about this all you want, but the fact remains. Either slim down or go home."

So it had come to this. Shape up or ship out. "Do you have any advice for me?" I asked meekly.

"Schedule more sessions with our trainer, take the stairs instead of the elevator, don't snack between meals," she said, ticking advice off on her fingertips. Why is it that whenever someone dispenses weight-loss advice they always make it so obvious? Like I didn't know that exercise was an important component of keeping fit. I was well aware of the importance of being in top form. That was why I devoted six days a week to Pilates, spinning, and running. My body has never been so problematic before. The problem had to be the blood.

"Do you think becoming a vampire has slowed down my metabolism?" I asked.

"I think you're looking for an excuse," said Iris. "Of all the physiological changes the vamp transition causes, I've never once heard of metabolic function being affected. I think you're grasping at straws here, Veronika."

"But I just don't see how that's possible. I haven't changed anything about my lifestyle. The only difference is now I'm a vamp instead of a human. That's just got to be what's causing—"

"None of the other girls have this problem," Iris cut me off. "Mindy, Liv, Laura B. None of them have gained so much as an ounce since being changed. In fact Laura B.'s body is hotter than ever. We've just booked her on three jobs in Japan for next week."

Swell.

"You, on the other hand," Iris said, paging through my file, "are not booked for anything."

I cringed. "But I thought you said I was just hitting a little bit of a lull. You said all models go through this."

"They do. But in your case it's becoming less of a lull, more of a fat problem. I don't want to hurt your feelings, sweetie, but you're getting to that stage where no designers and editors are going to use you. You're becoming too fat to be a plus-sized model."

There. She'd said it. "I appreciate your honesty," I said flatly. I felt hopeless and discouraged. All my warm feelings from seeing Jackson had evaporated into thin air. My mother's words flashed into my mind. *If you keep eating that way, your modeling career is going to be over before it starts.* When she'd said that to me in the airport six weeks ago, I'd laughed it off. I hadn't taken her seriously. It was ironic, really. My body—which had gotten me to New York in the first place—was going to be my undoing.

"I'll give it my absolute best shot," I promised, as I stood up to go. "This opportunity means the world to me. I don't want to ruin my chances."

I'd made it halfway to the door when Iris stopped me. "You know, there is one thing we could try," she mused. "I'm not sure how successful it would be, since we've never done it before."

I inched back into the room.

"I can't promise it will work, but what if we tried getting your, uh, nourishment from a different source?"

Uh-oh. I wasn't sure I liked the sound of that.

"All of the girls are drinking the exact same O-positive blood. But what if we got you something a little different?"

"Do you mean different, like I'm going to be drinking blood from a rat or a mosquito or something?" I asked, horrified at the thought.

"No, no, nothing like that. I was just thinking that we should make sure the blood you get is less fatty. Like if we take it from only the slimmest, fittest individuals. And then maybe dilute it with water, just to thin it out a bit."

Hmm. It seemed like a logical step. "Okay, I like it," I said, smiling broadly.

"Great! I'll take care of it ASAP," Iris assured me. "Just make sure you keep up your daily workouts and don't eat another drop until I have replacement supply sent over. Got it?"

"Got it," I said, waving good-bye as I headed downstairs to meet Jackson.

HE WAS NOT AS HAPPY TO SEE ME AS I WOULD have hoped.

"You're late," Jackson said irritably. "I've been waiting for nearly half an hour."

"I'm sorry," I apologized. "Iris D'Abruzzo had to discuss some important business with me."

"I understand sometimes these things can't be helped," Jackson said, "but now it looks like we've got an audience."

I could see the paparazzi stationed outside the door, waiting to snap pictures of our departure.

"Do you think someone tipped them off?" he asked. "They always seem to be one step ahead of us. I wonder if one of the low-level staffers at Vamp or Interscope is feeding them clues from our schedules?"

"Could be," I said. I'd wondered about this myself from time to time. "Or maybe it's just a Gawker Stalker feature."

"There's also this," he said, reaching into his pocket and pulling out a folded up magazine clipping.

It was from the current issue of *Us Weekly*, which hit newsstands that day.

"Read it," Jackson said.

I stared down at the page. It was an article. About me! The headline read, "Vamp Veronika a Real Bloodsucker."

I gasped. "What is this?"

"Just read it."

I skimmed the article. The first sentence read, *"Chubette model Veronika James is known for her vicious, vamplike ways both in front of the camera and off. Childhood friend Kerry Malone said, 'Veronika's known around town for being devious and manipulative. It's also totally fitting that she joined an agency called Vamp, considering she's obsessed with the underworld and frequently dresses up as a member of the undead. She used to come to school dolled up like Mrs. Dracula, with fake fangs and a black cape and everything.'"*

"KERRY MALONE!" I shrieked. "We're not friends. We hate each other. And that story is so dumb! Yes, I went to school dressed as a vampire one time. But it was in the sixth grade, for Halloween!" I was fuming.

Jackson stared at the ground. "Look Veronika, I hate to do this, but I really have to go. I have a plane to catch," he said, uncomfortably. "I'm gonna be away for a few days. But when I get back . . . well, I'm not so sure this is going to work out between us."

"What!" I exclaimed. "Because of this dumb article?"

He sighed. "It's not just that," he said. "But, well, I'm a pretty traditional guy. I have traditional values. And this dabbling in the occult thing is a little weird. It doesn't sit right with me."

"But I'm not dabbling in the occult," I said, rather unconvincingly, I might add.

"Your attitude has been weird, too. You never eat. You're so pale. You stay out all night long at the clubs. I just don't know if that's what I want in a girlfriend. I'm sorry."

Girlfriend. Oh my God. Jackson Lowe had just called me his girlfriend. Past tense. I didn't realize he'd viewed us that way. I didn't even know I had him. Until I lost him.

Jackson gave me a quick peck on the cheek good-bye, and then headed out of the lobby and into his waiting car. With tears streaming down my face, I ran back upstairs to seek solace in Iris's office. I didn't want to see her again, didn't really feel like having another weight-centric conversation. But it beat the hell out of going outside and facing the waiting paparazzi.

I HAD TO FIND DEX. HE WAS THE ONLY ONE WHO could help me.

I'd been reading up about vampires, separating the fact from fiction. And one thing became clear. The only way to undo what had been done—the only way to change me back from a vamp to a mortal—was with Dex's help.

Since he had turned me, there was a chance he could reverse me. It was possible that too much time had passed. According to my research, with each passing day it got harder and harder to go back. The longer I stayed a vamp, the more it got into my blood stream.

And make no mistake about it: I did want to go back. And not just to being a human being, either. I wanted to be a normal girl. At home with my parents, out of the tabloids, and into the normal, ordinary world of a soon-to-be high school senior.

My mother and father had been calling for days, begging me to drop out of the program and come back to Mildew. They were freaked out by all of the media coverage, and they worried that I'd get mixed up in something bad.

Ha! They didn't know the half of it.

NINE

DEX WAS GONE. I WAS SURE OF IT. IT HAD BEEN two weeks since I'd last seen him. He'd been hanging out in Europe, doing fashion spreads, and presumably, recruiting other vampires.

If he didn't come back soon I'd be screwed.

As it stood, Jackson wasn't talking to me. He'd been refusing to take my calls, refusing to give me the time of day. I wanted to make things right between us again.

On a positive note, I'd managed to lose seven of the thirteen pounds I gained. Despite my new low-fat, low-calorie blood diet, the weight was only sluggishly coming off. It figured. As usual it was easier to put weight on than to take it off.

I searched for Dex for weeks before he finally turned up. I ambushed him at one of Iris's parties, pleaded my case, and begged him for help.

"Why do you want out so bad?" Dex asked, laughing. "I've given you a gift, the best gift anyone could ask for. You get to stay young and beautiful forever. Do you know how much money people spend on plastic surgery and stupid creams just to try to capture their youth?"

"It's Jackson," I told him, sobbing. "I have to do it or I won't be able to be with him anymore."

Dex listened intently, as I told him about the terrible articles and the mean former friends and the way Jackson had deserted me. I told him about the research I'd done, how I knew it was possible that he could change me back over. I couldn't tell if it was working, couldn't tell if I was having any effect on him at all.

"So you really want to be with this guy? It means that much to you?"

"Yes," I said. "It means everything."

Then he smiled and said, "Give me a few days. I might be able to take care of this for you."

$\mathfrak{I}$T WAS FOUR DAYS LATER WHEN I HEARD FROM Dex again.

In the meantime, I tried desperately to get a hold of Jackson. I called his cell repeatedly, e-mailed him numerous times—nothing. I thought he was avoiding me. But then Jackson's agent called and told me he'd been MIA for the past few days.

"It's like he's evaporated into thin air," he told me. "No one has seen or heard from him in almost a week."

I grew insane with fear. As soon as I finished talking to Jackson's manager, there was a knock at the door.

I flung it open. "Jackson!" I screamed, as he came inside. "Thank God! I was just talking to your manager. We thought something awful had happened. I was two seconds away from filing a missing person's report."

He was pale and thin and, instinctively, I moved forward to embrace him. He didn't pull back, didn't say anything.

And then it happened. The most horrible, awful thing I could imagine.

Jackson smiled really wide, revealing two sharp, shiny fangs.

"I told you," Dex said, coming in the door behind him. "I told you I would sort this out."

"No!" I screamed, realizing what he'd done.

Jackson still didn't say anything. He looked dazed, tired.

"Just a few quick bites of the neck and all was well. Now you can be together forever," Dex said, with a twinkle in his eye. "I turned him into a vampire, just for you."

"You can't!" I wailed. "You've destroyed him, destroyed his career. He'll never be the same old Jackson." I thought about all of his wonderful qualities—the sweetness, the sensitivity. They would be gone now.

"He won't be the same," Dex said, "that's true. He'll be better."

"But you should have left him alone."

"And spoil all the fun?" Dex laughed. "Now he gets to live forever."

Jackson, who had been standing there quietly, broke into a large grin. "Come on, Veronika," he said. "Let's go out. I'm hungry." He licked his lips and started for the door.

Sydney's Story

—●●—

SERENA ROBAR

ONE

I PLOPPED DOWN IN FIRST CLASS AND SIGHED sweetly. I could stretch my legs all the way out. I'd been six one since the sixth grade and no seats ever worked for me. I pulled out my *Hipster Chick* magazine and started to thumb through it.

"Sydney Turner?" one of the flight attendants interrupted.

"Yes?"

"I'm sorry to bother you, but I have to ask. That's you, right? The model search contest winner?" She pointed to the magazine with my picture and several other winners emblazed on the cover.

"Yeah. One of them anyway." I smiled, a bit embarrassed to be recognized on the plane.

"So were you really discovered waiting in line with your friend? You had no intention of entering the contest yourself?"

"Yeah, Katy should be here, not me." I shook my head in wonder.

"Was she mad when they picked you instead of her?"

That was a tougher question to answer. At first Katy'd been shocked, but when she realized I had no intention of going with the photographer and getting my picture taken, she rallied. Katy went from disappointed entrant to manager of my modeling career in the span of three minutes.

"She was surprisingly cool about it. Very insistent that I go to New York for the summer."

She'd actually browbeaten and threatened me within an inch of my life to accept the prize. Three months in New York City modeling for Vamp Modeling Inc. It took appealing to my practical side to finally give in. She thought I might earn enough money to cover at least a year of college.

The attendant patted my shoulder in a congratulatory sort of way. "Good for you. Friends like that are hard to find. Be sure to get her something nice while you're in the city. Maybe you can convince a designer to give you a free purse or something for your friend?" she suggested with a wink.

"Yeah, Katy gave me a list. She wants anything from Fendi and Ferragamo and I am not to return to Seattle without Lindsay Lohan's autograph."

We shared a laugh over Katy's wish list, and she brought

me a soda as well as a movie player. It was pretty slick and time passed quickly.

It was a six-hour flight from Seattle to NYC and I was the first to disembark with my heavy carry-on. The flight crew wished me luck and asked me to sign the issue of *HC* magazine. I felt weird, but they made such a fuss I couldn't say no.

Dad had promised to meet me in the terminal. It seemed strange that my dad was here for the summer, too, but it was probably the only way my mom would let me come. He was working at the headquarters of a new corporate law firm and then going back to Seattle to open a satellite office. This new firm was very respectable and only the top lawyers were considered.

I wondered how this "respectable firm" felt about a man chucking out his first wife and marrying a woman half his age.

I found him easily enough, as he was tall like me. I got Mom's delicate features and big eyes but Dad's lanky build. Not sure where the lack of curves fit into the picture. Hardly seemed fair to give me size twelve feet and skimp on the boobs.

My smile of greeting froze on my face when I saw Brittani waiting with Dad, looking delighted to be preggers in her designer maternity-ware. Brittani was so physically fit, she looked like she had a soccer ball taped to her stomach. Not an ounce of excess fat anywhere. It was creepy.

"Well, don't you look . . . ?" Brittani trailed off as she sought the right phrase, her lips pursed in disapproval. Dad's mouth tightened as well. Jackpot! Double whammy and I'd only *just* stepped off the plane. So glad I took the time to henna tattoo my stomach to draw attention to my new belly-button ring.

"I miss your long hair," my father finally said, pointedly ignoring its blue color as well as my tattooed tummy and military cargo pants tucked into biker boots.

"It's good to see you, too, Dad," I replied sarcastically.

He ignored the razor edge to my voice and started to walk toward baggage claim. Brittani fell in step with him and I followed behind.

Dad addressed me from over his shoulder. "I promised your mother I would ensure you conduct yourself like a proper young lady while doing this contest thing." His lips compressed into a tight line again.

Hey bonus! Dad hated the idea of me modeling for the summer. Right on.

"Really?" I asked skeptically. "Mom was concerned I would embarrass the family my first time away from home?"

"I think what your father is trying to say is New York can be very seductive especially for a young girl so easily led astray."

"So easily led astray?" I parroted back. Witch!

She nodded enthusiastically, as though I was agreeing with her. It took all my willpower not to say, "You mean like sleeping with a married guy and breaking up his family?" Although Dad still insisted he didn't start dating Brittani until after he and Mom split up. I suppose I'd be required to act surprised when the baby, or the Usurper as I referred to it, arrived "early" as well.

But that kind of comment guaranteed a scene in the middle of the airport and I hardly wanted my first meeting with Vamp Modeling Inc.'s liaison, Marlena Stuart, to consist of a screaming match in public with my dad. Although I couldn't resist commenting, "I'm just here to earn money for school."

"Well, just don't let me find you inside the pages of *Playboy* the minute you turn eighteen," my father said stiffly.

"Why, Daddy!" I declared in mock horror. "You shouldn't be looking at *Playboy*."

We walked the rest of the way to baggage claim in silence. I couldn't believe he thought I'd bare it all the minute I turned eighteen. I'd never done anything the least bit unsuitable until he dumped his family and started a new one.

"Sydney darling!" A woman in her late twenties waved from across the baggage terminal. Behind her stood a small group of camera-wearing men and women. We made our way toward them and the area blazed with flashes, causing everyone in the immediate vicinity to look our way and speculate who we were.

The chic blonde who called my name stepped forward and embraced me. Not with a fake hug like I gave Brittani, but a hug that seemed to say she was genuinely thrilled I had arrived.

"I am Marlena, dear. So wonderful to meet you at last."

She immediately shook my father's hand and said, "And there is no doubting who this handsome man is. Sydney had to get her fabulous looks from somewhere. Charmed to meet you."

I watched in awe as my father practically stuttered his greeting and actually blushed. Marlena Stuart was the coolest. Dad introduced Brittani.

"I'm sure you feel blessed having such a talented stepdaughter. Your child will grow up to idolize Sydney, of course. As will half the teens in America."

Scratch that, Marlena was now my biggest hero. The look on Brittani's face when she said her kid would idolize me was priceless.

"Everyone, everyone." Marlena clapped her hands together to get the attention of the press. "This is the new face of fashion. Behold Miss Sydney Turner. Get used to this face, people. You're going to be seeing a lot of it."

TWO

ONCE WE WERE ALONE IN THE LIMO, I SORT OF disintegrated into the seat.

"Tired?" she asked kindly.

"Mentally exhausted. Dealing with my dad is like . . ." I struggled for the right words but couldn't find them. "I don't know." I finished lamely. "You sure shook him up though," I added. "I've never seen him anything but totally self assured. You had him blushing like a schoolboy."

Marlena dug through some sort of minifridge in the limo—how cool was that?—as she answered, "Men are not so difficult to manipulate when you know the right buttons to push."

She handed me a glass flute, then wrestled with a bottle

of champagne. The sudden pop of the cork shooting free made me laugh.

"Bring your glass here, hurry, before we make a mess."

I quickly tipped the glass under the flowing spout to fill it. She did the same for herself, then put the bottle in a bucket of ice.

"You know I'm not twenty-one," I blurted, in a very nonhip way. *Great, now she'd think I was the biggest prude on the face of the planet, despite the blue hair.*

"Relax, your dad isn't here and a toast is in order. Let me see. Ah yes. To new beginnings."

I echoed her sentiment. We clinked glasses and I took a tentative sip. I knew right away I'd never learn to love the taste of this fizzy, bitter drink. Marlena laughed at my expression and took the glass away.

"It's an acquired taste," she assured me, taking another sip.

"It'd have to be." I motioned toward the minifridge.

"Help yourself," she said.

I found a Mountain Dew (is there a more perfect drink on the planet? I don't think so) to wash away the taste of champagne.

Marlena pulled a folder out of her bag. "Your summer is going to be packed. Here's your schedule. The events listed in blue are your shoots and the red ones are promos you're required to attend. Those in green are optional. That is to say, we'd like you to make it to those events but understand you are only human. However the red and blue ones are mandatory. You can see you'll be very busy this summer with little downtime. I will see you at some of the shoots and promos, and you can always reach me by cell phone. I have assigned you a bodyguard for the red promos."

"Oh no, Marlena, I don't need a bodyguard. I won't get into any trouble, I promise."

It seemed totally unnecessary to assign me some big, hairy guy to glare menacingly at anyone around me. If I didn't stick out before, having Guido the Bodyguard would surely seal the deal and I said as much.

"Darling, a bodyguard is trés chic! Paris Hilton has one. Only the top of the food chain need a bodyguard. It's perfect for your image. The bad girl and her bodyguard. What will she do next? The press will have a field day speculating."

"Uh, bad girl?" I was confused. "What are you talking about?"

"My darling Sydney, you're the 'bad' girl. I am pitching you to the press as the wild child. The girl with a chip on her shoulder, who has her own style and doesn't compromise."

"But, Marlena, I'm not like that at all."

"Really?" She raised an eyebrow in disbelief. "Then what's with the dog collar, nose ring, and blue hair? Your whole outfit screams rebel, Sydney dear. If you're not marching to the beat of your own drum, what are you doing?"

When I was in private school, my dad always prided himself on what a clean-cut girl I was. He loved my long chestnut hair. When he left my mom, I decided to show my displeasure by cutting it short.

When I discovered he left her for a twenty-six-year-old personal trainer named Brittani (that's Brittani with an *I*), I dyed sections of it electric blue. When he announced she was pregnant, I pierced my nose.

And when he announced he couldn't afford to pay for college after purchasing a two million dollar condo overlooking Puget Sound for his new family, I pierced my belly button.

My lips tightened and I looked away, trying to hide the tears welling up in my eyes.

"Oh," Marlena said softly, "I think I get it now. You were Daddy's little girl and now Daddy has a whole new family."

She didn't say it unkindly but the words stung nonetheless. I *had* been Daddy's little girl. All my life I strove to be perfect for him, to live up to his expectations. I'd been a perfect little girl and he'd left us anyway.

Marlena grabbed my hands and held them with hers. "It's okay, Sydney. I understand. Good for you, having the gumption to fight back the only way you can."

Tears fell down my cheeks and I'm sure a long smudge of eyeliner followed. Marlena understood me. She wasn't judging my actions or telling me I was only hurting myself. She was applauding my efforts. If I didn't already think she rocked, she just achieved legendary status in my eyes.

"Maybe we could turn this whole thing into a win-win situation for both of us?"

"Wh-what do you mean?" I sniffed and she handed me a tissue from some compartment behind her. Was there anything this limo didn't have handy?

"Well, I need a bad girl for the press to write about. Someone outrageous and unpredictable. Someone Page Six–worthy. You want to punish your dad and embarrass him."

When she said it like that, it sounded childish and petty so I interrupted her. "It's not that I am trying to punish him. . . ."

"Pish, posh, Sydney. Of course you are. Lying to yourself about your true intentions is childish. Knowing what you want and doing what is necessary to achieve it is mature and freeing. You can't be Daddy's little girl forever and it looks like Brittani is well on the way to replacing you, so the time for children's games is over."

Her eyes got hard and it kind of freaked me out when she talked like that. But she was right. I wasn't a little girl anymore. I *had* changed my appearance to get back at Dad. I did it to hurt him. It was childish of me not to acknowledge that. It was the truth.

"So what are you suggesting?"

"Play the part of the bad girl! Go wild or at least look like you're going wild. I can see you aren't the type to completely go off the deep end, but you appear to have good acting skills. Make the world think you're Sydney Turner, the girl who cannot be tamed by anyone."

"So you want me to misbehave at shoots and stuff?" I was totally confused.

"No, no. You must be a professional at all the blue appointments. Nothing excites the press more than a wild child who still manages to work and succeed, despite her partying ways." Marlena laughed. "This is where our plan is brilliant. You won't really be drinking until all hours and sleeping around. You'll just *appear* to have the wild social life. Who's to know the drink in your glass is ginger ale and not whisky and tonic? Once the ball starts rolling, PR will link up-and-coming actors and male models to you for the exposure. You won't have to do anything but dance with them or talk to them at clubs. The press will make up the rest."

"Why would anyone believe it?" I questioned. It seemed ridiculous that anyone who knew me would believe I could change so completely in a single summer. My mom would certainly never buy it. But what about the people in New York who didn't know me?

"Because I will deny, deny, deny. If someone links you to Colin Farrell I will say, 'Certainly not. Sydney only spoke to Mr. Farrell briefly. Nothing illicit is going on.' Then we make sure you're seen talking with Mr. Farrell at another function. The press will be all over it. See? It's all subterfuge!"

"You are going to try to get me linked to Colin Farrell?" I asked stupidly.

She waved her hand dismissively in the air. "That's just an example. We only have three months so I'm not making any promises about him. We'll have to start out with up-and-comers. Those who are hungry for exposure. We're fortunate because Vamp Modeling is all about the PR machine and will have the press following you constantly. It's part of the contest promotion. Good for Vamp Modeling and good for *Hipster Chick* magazine, which will be covering the antics of the winners of the contest. It's perfect! Well, what do you think?"

"You know, Marlena. You are one scary chick when you get hold of an idea," I said slowly.

She laughed. "Darling Sydney, you do this right and you'll earn more than enough college money. You'll be the hottest ticket in town and can model for as long as you want."

I did need the college money. I dreamed of going to art school someday.

"Sydney?" Marlena coaxed, when I grew thoughtful. "Do we have a plan?"

"Yeah." I cleared my throat and said it more definitively. "Yeah, we have a plan."

THREE

We ARRIVED AT THE RITZ, YES, THE FREAKIN'
Ritz, where I would live for the summer. I was a bit disappointed that I only had an interior room with no outside
view, but the luxurious lobby and splendor made up for
the lack of scenery. The Ritz was a New York icon and I
was living the dream. I was minutes away from the best
shopping in the world. How cool was I?

I had several hours before a car would pick me up for
our first "thing" at 10:00 P.M. in the Village, so I decided to
order room service. After my hamburger arrived—yeah,
not very original of me but I like hamburgers—someone
dropped off an outfit Marlena sent over for me to wear that

night. I pulled the plastic off anxiously and almost had a heart attack.

Oh. My. Gosh. There was no way I could wear this thing. Attending an all-girl private school with uniforms had not prepared me for this. I mean I wanted to make Marlena happy since she'd gone to the trouble of sending me an outfit, but I wasn't ready to attack the world in a belted mini that probably wouldn't cover my butt and a top that looked suspiciously like a scarf.

I gave up trying to figure out the top and logged on to the Internet from my laptop. I wanted to get an idea of where I was going. Surely the Village had a flavor or reputation that would help me dress the part.

Hmm, let's see. Lots of tattoo and piercing places, Beatnik influences. Known for its nightlife. I might not know Greenwich Village but I knew Capitol Hill in Seattle and they sounded very similar. I could totally dress for a night out on Capitol Hill.

My confidence returned further after I'd scrubbed off the airplane smell. Getting ready was a long process. The electric blue hair was longer than the rest, but all of my hair was shaped with a long razor to give it that ragged-edged look. It required lots of gel. I applied eyeliner like it was going out of style and just a light coat of loose powder to give my clear skin a glow. My green eyes stood out from across the room.

I pulled on the mini and disregarded the scarf top. Instead I opted for a worn black retro concert tank and pulled on an old pair of fishnet nylons. They were ripped but added character to my look. Especially since I wore them with biker boots. I cinched the thick belt and looked in the mirror.

Who was this girl? I wondered as I stared at my reflection.

The front desk called and informed me my car had arrived. I left my room, tucking the key into my purse. I rushed to the elevators and rode down without incident, though I noticed a lot of stares when I crossed the lobby. Sure, I might be ready for the Village, but I certainly wasn't dressed for the Ritz.

Several cars were in the valet area, but one had the hottest guy I'd ever seen standing next to it. Dark brown hair touched his collar in a very sexy way. He was taller than me, I realized with a happy sigh, and built like a football player. That was one fine solid-looking chest beneath that crisp white knit shirt. He was talking on his cell phone.

Our eyes met, and he slowly pulled the phone away from his ear and flipped it closed. I'd never seen eyes so mesmerizing before. They were liquid amber and though he was easily four car lengths away, I knew they'd have specks of brown and black in them. If this was Guido the Bodyguard, I'd wear whatever stupid outfit Marlena sent me with no questions asked for the next three months. He was beautiful and he would be sticking by my side for the whole summer. Yeah me.

He strode purposefully toward me and I took an involuntary step back. Why? I have no idea. He was just so powerful that I needed to step back to absorb his presence. Does that make sense?

"Sydney Turner?" he asked, and I nodded dumbly. His voice even sounded powerful. He couldn't have been more than twenty but he seemed older. My mom would call it an old soul. I never really knew what she meant until now. He seemed almost world-weary.

"My name is Carl and I'm your Guido for the evening."

I laughed and my tension melted away. "Nice to meet you." I pumped his hand enthusiastically, looking him straight in the eye. "I'm your 'bad' girl for the evening."

He raised an eyebrow and I blushed, realizing how that sounded. I figured if Marlena had told him the Guido joke, she must have filled him in on our plan. From the look on his face, apparently not.

"I mean, I need a bodyguard so I must be a bad girl." I stammered and blushed even deeper when he raised his eyebrows at my explanation. His mouth twitched, as though fighting a smile.

"No," I blurted out, horrified, "I mean, I mean . . ." I stopped digging myself a bigger, deeper hole and took a ragged breath, shook my arms out by my side and looked down at the ground.

Then I started over, smiling as I looked him in the eye and put out my hand again, pretending we just met. "Hi, my name is Sydney Turner, and I am very happy to meet you."

He chuckled and when he shook my hand it was surprisingly cool for such a warm night but I felt a charge of electricity running down to my boots from his touch. If he felt the same, he didn't show it, though I bet he could hear my heart racing because I felt the pounding of blood in my ears.

"Shall we go?" He stepped back and motioned toward the black Town Car. He gently touched the small of my back to guide me to the car, but his hand on me made me stumble. I quickly righted myself, even as his other hand moved to support me.

He opened the back door and I stood in a moment of indecision. "Would it make me terribly uncouth if I wanted to ride in the front seat with you? I've never been to New York and I'm sure I'll be asking a ton of questions and you'll be constantly talking over your shoulder so I can hear you, and well, it might be safer and easier if I rode shotgun?"

I hoped I didn't sound like a hick but I didn't want to sit behind him. I wanted to look at his profile and talk to him as a person, not from the back of a car seat, like he was my dad dropping me off at the mall.

He stared at me a moment, then rewarded me with a sparkling smile. "Miss Turner, you're nothing at all like I expected and I would be delighted to have such a charming companion ride shotgun."

I smiled as he held open the door. Sliding into the passenger seat, I said, "Please call me Sydney or Syd." I looked back up at him once I was settled and added, "You know, you shouldn't judge a book by its cover."

He held the door a moment longer and replied, "I believe covers on books are designed to tell as much about the book as possible, to entice a potential reader to open them up."

That was about the sexiest analogy I'd ever heard and I felt like begging him to read me. What was happening here? I'd never thought things like that before. "Maybe its time you visited a new library?" I quipped and he laughed again.

"This assignment looks to be the most enjoyable one I've had in a long time, Sydney." And he closed the door.

FOUR

"YOU ARE THE MOST TROUBLESOME ASSIGNMENT I've ever had," Carl stated as he all but threw me in the back of the car.

"You can't blame me for what happened in there!" I exclaimed when he slid into the driver's seat to start the car.

"You started a brawl between two boys," Carl reminded me angrily, gunning the motor.

"I didn't start anything. They were the ones who had too much to drink. They were acting like idiots. I was minding my own busi—"

"Don't you dare tell me you were minding your own business. You were dancing and cavorting with both of them all evening and they were only trying to match you drink for drink!"

I felt a twinge of guilt at that reminder. I was, indeed, sucking down the drinks, which to the uneducated observer looked suspiciously like mixed drinks. Marlena set up a tab for all the contestants but I had ordered ginger ale with a lime twist. I just told the bartender to keep them coming.

The two young men in question joined me after my second drink, so they assumed it was alcohol and, not to be outdone by a mere girl, tried to match my intake. I was supposed to be the "bad" girl so I couldn't correct them. The press had captured the entire scene when one of the guys tried to cut in on the other on the dance floor.

Carl broke it up and then swept me away from harm by throwing my butt into the back of the Town Car to avoid further mishaps. I was totally innocent, but I couldn't tell Carl that. If Marlena hadn't filled him in on the plan, she must have wanted everything to look as real as possible. Now Carl thought I was some boozing flirt who egged on men to fight for me. But Marlena was thrilled with the brawl and gave me the thumbs-up sign as Carl dragged me to the car.

I sighed melodramatically and looked out the window. The bright city lights flashed by as we drove. It was two in the morning New York time, so five in the morning for me. I was bone tired but more than that, I was hungry. I usually carried some crackers or something in my purse because

I suffered from low blood sugar, but the purse I used tonight was too small.

I looked at the rearview mirror and inquired hesitantly, "Carl?"

"What?" he snapped back.

"Do you think we could, uh, hit a drive-thru or something? I'm kind of hungry."

"You want food?" he restated dumbly.

"Uh, yeah. I'm actually kind of starving. Isn't New York famous for its late-night restaurants?" I leaned forward in the seat so that I was closer to him, forgetting his earlier annoyance with me. I loved food. People thought because I was so skinny, I never ate but that was so not true. I ate a lot and all the time. I know it didn't sound fair, but I had a hard time keeping weight on.

Two years ago, Mom took me to a doctor because she thought there was something seriously wrong with me. No one, she said to the doctor, can eat as much as I could and not gain weight. They ran a whole bunch of tests but in the end I only had a freakishly high metabolism. The doctor suggested taking up weight training to keep my muscles strong and to keep eating. So I did eat. Every chance I could.

"You're telling me a model as rail thin as you is starving?"

"What's that supposed to mean? Models can't get hungry?"

"Of course they can. They just usually don't eat or they recycle after they binge."

"That's a very prejudiced thing to say. How many models do you know, anyway?" I wished I could take back the question the minute it slipped from my lips. The thought of Carl knowing any models didn't make me very happy. Which was stupid since I just met the guy.

"You mean as well as I know you?"

I rolled my eyes. "Yeah, as deeply and thoroughly as you know me."

His lip twitched, trying to hold back a smile. "Well, none actually."

I laughed at his admission. "There you go then."

Carl turned the tables on me. "How many do you know?"

"Well, none actually." He laughed again and I joined him. "Okay, so we can agree that neither of us are experts on the eating practices of models but can we agree that *this* model is starving and needs to be fed?"

"Sounds fair. What kind of food do you like?"

"Hmm, I kind of like everything. What do you like?" I asked him, once again leaning up to watch him through the rearview mirror.

Carl grew silent and I thought for a moment he didn't hear me when he said flatly, "Anything. Pick what you like."

I frowned at him, puzzled by the abrupt way we went from friendly banter to his now tight-lipped expression. I guess he wasn't willing to let bygones be bygones from earlier tonight. But that didn't change the fact that I was hungry.

"Let's do Chinese food. The girls on *Sex and the City* always do Chinese takeout."

"Are you telling me everything you know about the greatest city on Earth has been learned by watching television?"

I defended myself. "Dude, not just television. HBO."

"Well, then. I stand corrected." He continued to expertly maneuver through the streets and flipped open his cell phone. Within moments, he placed an order for a little bit of everything. My mouth watered at the thought of all that food.

He found a place with no difficulty and grabbed our order, then returned us to the Ritz in record time. I was confused when he stopped the car in front of the door but left the motor running.

"Aren't you coming in?"

"Look at the time, Sydney. It's hardly appropriate for me to go to your room at this hour of the night."

"But what about all this food? Should we just divide it up?" I was disappointed he didn't want to share our feast.

"No, you take it. My treat. I'll see you next time."

I gathered all the wonderful smelling containers and scooted out the open door. "I can't possibly eat all of this." I wouldn't beg him to have dinner with me. Even I had some dignity. At least, I hoped so.

We looked at each other a long moment before he finally shook his head. "It's very late or very early in the morning, depending on how you look at it. You have a full day to-morrow and don't need me keeping you up any later."

I nodded my head in agreement. I did have a long day tomorrow. At least I'd see him again at my next red appointment. I made my way up to the room and gorged myself on Chinese food until I couldn't eat another bite. That might have been the best meal ever. I double-checked my schedule and cringed when I noticed the start time. Ugh. I'd only get a few hours of sleep.

I requested a wake-up call and dreamed of Carl's laughter and pork fried rice.

FIVE

I ARRIVED AT MY FIRST MODELING ASSIGNMENT with a food hangover. Never again. I was puffy from all the sodium and MSG and had a headache. I'm sure everyone would assume I'd partied all night but the real culprit was Szechwan chicken.

Marlena was there to greet me. "Darling, you look positively exhausted."

"Jet lag," I told her.

"Yes, yes. It was pure evil of me to have you get started so soon after arriving but it's a very short session today, then you can go take a nap before tonight."

"Tonight?" I asked.

"Of course, darling. We have another thing. This time

in Midtown. Won't take but an hour. You'll be in bed in no time."

My first modeling job was relatively easy. No need to do hair and makeup, as the only thing being photographed was my back. Actually I was modeling low-rise jeans. The makeup girl applied a fake tattoo to most of my lower back, and the pants, well, the pants covered less area than the tattoo.

The photographer asked me to "assume the position" against a brick wall. Huh? Marlena explained they wanted me to put my hands up on the wall and spread my legs as though I was being frisked by the police. I wore the jeans, a halter top with small straps, and a pair of really high heels that were mostly obscured by the pants.

I couldn't believe that such jeans existed. Not because they were so low but because the legs were so long and they still fit. And they fit like a glove. A glove with a serious "coin slot" but a glove nonetheless. I was glad my face wouldn't be in the picture.

I was told to arch my back, not so much, stick out my butt, more, yes, that's it. Flex your bottom. I started laughing, which earned me a quick *shush* from the photographer. "Okay, now lose the top."

What?!

Marlena saw my panic and explained the situation. "Sydney dear, they want some shots without the halter straps. Nothing will show in the photograph."

Screw that! What about all the people in the room?

I didn't want to let Marlena down but I didn't want to take off my top, either. I looked around and there were only a couple of other people, and all were women, so it wasn't any different than being in the school locker room, right?

I nodded and undid the straps, covering myself modestly as I handed the shirt to Marlena. I slowly put my hands back up on the brick wall and squeezed my eyes shut. I heard the shutter whirl, arched my back, pushed out my butt, and all those asinine things they asked before and then they were done. Marlena handed me a robe and praised my efforts. I went back to the makeshift changing room to switch back into my clothes and was surprised to find my hands trembling.

When I won the contest, my best friend, Katy, asked me if I was going to pose without a top on and I assured her that I, Sydney Turner, took my top off for no photographer. No matter what. And in the blink of an eye, I'd crossed a line I never thought I would. Sure, no one would ever know that was me in the ad, and I didn't show my breasts or anything, but I did something I swore to myself I never would. I just wasn't sure how to deal with it.

"Great news, Sydney darling," Marlena called to me from behind the curtain. "The jeans are yours to keep. One of the perks of this job. Nice, huh?"

"Yeah, thanks." I looked down at the jeans. The perfect jeans that actually fit my body and were long enough to wear with high heels and what they symbolized. I wondered if I could ever bring myself to wear them again.

Carl picked me up for the next "thing," and I was well rested. A nice long nap, a refreshing hot shower, and the prospect of seeing him again had restored my good humor. I once again dressed the part of the bad girl, this time with less dog collar. Carl waited patiently by my side as I hobnobbed with Marlena and some local politicians. At one point I thought a district representative actually pinched my bottom, but I couldn't be sure.

We left the shindig at close to one in the morning. The mere hour Marlena promised me had drug out to three. When I got back in the car next to Carl, he tossed a newspaper at me.

"What's this?" I asked.

"It's called a newspaper," he deadpanned.

"Hardy har har. No, I mean why are you giving it to me?"

He looked surprised. "Don't all you model types live for Page Six in the *Post*?"

"Hardly."

Carl shook his head in amazement. "It's the gossip section. The who's who of New York is listed there. What they are doing, where they were seen."

"So why would I be interested?"

"Because you're in it."

I quickly turned the paper to Page Six and sure enough, last night's tussle was listed with a photograph. You couldn't see my face but it was a great picture of the guy on the floor, holding a bloody nose.

> Vamp Modeling bad girl, Sydney Turner, had oil-tycoon heir William Farr III and up-and-coming actor Tag Miller coming to blows at the opening of Club Vintage in the Village last night.

"Oh my," I said.

"That photo doesn't do you justice, by the way," Carl commented.

"I highly doubt it was supposed to. I think it was meant to humiliate Bill. It's a great shot of his bloody nose, don't you think?"

I held it up for him to see and he glanced my way. "It doesn't bother you that you weren't featured more prominently?"

I thought about the plan for a moment then shrugged my shoulders. "They mentioned the agency so that should make Marlena happy. Other than that, not really."

What would Dad say once he read Page Six? But what were the odds he would read the gossip column? Now, Brittani, on the other hand . . .

"I just don't get you, Sydney Turner." Carl shook his head.

"My mom tells me a woman should create a little mystery. Never reveal too much," I teased. Actually I was pretty sure Mom was referring to not having sex too soon in a relationship but I guess her advice worked in this situation, too.

"Do you want to walk around Central Park?" I blurted out, not wanting the night to end.

"Do you think that's wise at this time of night?" Carl asked.

It wasn't a "no," so I pressed on. "You look like a tough guy who can handle himself."

Actually it wasn't the smartest suggestion to advocate a stroll around Central Park at one in the morning but I felt safe with Carl. I wondered if he would hold my hand as we walked around. My fingers tingled at the thought.

At that moment we pulled up to the front of the Ritz.

"Another night then?" I queried lightheartedly, trying to hide my disappointment.

Carl didn't get out of the car and open my side like he usually did. We just sat in the running car, looking at each other. No words were spoken, but I felt like we were communicating all the same.

I wanted to look into his beautiful eyes forever, and unconsciously, I leaned forward. He smelled incredible. I felt some magnetic pull toward him. I couldn't describe it but at that moment, I wanted nothing more than to kiss his soft, firm mouth and feel his arms around me. I'd never felt such a powerful attraction before. It was almost supernatural in its intensity.

Carl broke the spell when I was a hairbreadth from his face. "Another time then."

I jerked back. Confused, I shook my head and mumbled a lame good night. I was out of the car before Carl had time to open my door. I'd never been so forward in my life. It was weird and so unlike me. I mean, Carl was hot and all but I barely knew him. We laughed and there was definitely chemistry but I wasn't the type of girl to kiss all the boys. I just wasn't. What was it with me and Carl anyway?

SIX

I SPENT MY DAY OFF SKETCHING COMICS AND wandering around Madison Avenue, window-shopping.

On Monday, I started modeling in earnest and my days took on a bizarre sort of pattern. I spent them at photo shoots, some lasting just a few short hours and some lasting days. I learned how to walk the catwalk for charity fashion shows and could recognize the photographers and their crew.

I became acquainted with other models, though no one ever seemed friendly enough to encourage me to hang with them outside of work. There were divas and bitches and everything in between. For the most part, I liked the people I met. They worked hard, possessed an artistic soul, and were looking to express themselves in some way.

As for myself, I spent my spare time drawing but missed the freedom of doodling at will. And the nights, the nights were met with a sort of anticipated dread. I counted the minutes until my phone would ring to announce Carl downstairs but I disliked the role I played while out at our "things," as we called them.

After my evening of inflaming usually sensible men to act like braying jackasses or making a point of getting a photo taken with so and so, I anxiously awaited the nod from Marlena that let me know I had done my duty and could go home.

Except it wasn't my room at the Ritz I longed for; it was the stolen moments with Carl in the car. Sometimes he took the long way home and we told stories and laughed. He loved to hear my take on the modeling world, and once I even showed him one of my comics. He begged to see more, and before I knew it, I took my sketchbook with me to "things" and left it in the car for us to review on the way home.

I wanted so much to see him outside of work, but he always politely declined my suggestions of meeting during the day, so I stopped asking. Maybe he worked, maybe he went to school, and maybe he truly wasn't interested in more than friendship. Either way, I didn't want to risk spoiling the precious little time I had with him, so I didn't push.

My father called me weekly, always after a story came out where he could chastise my behavior. Finally, about six weeks into my stay, he scheduled a lunch for us on a Saturday.

I was surprised, but I couldn't avoid him forever. He and Brittani picked me up and took me to a little restaurant on the Upper West Side.

After our meal, I sensed the small talk was at an end when my father asked, "So, Sydney, what are your plans after spending the summer in New York?"

He made it sound like I was on a holiday, like I was backpacking through Europe instead of working to pay for art school.

"Well, Dad, it's my hope to earn enough money this summer to pay for a year or two of school."

"I see, yes. What about community college? You could earn your AA and then go on to a larger university."

"That's something to consider," I stated carefully. "But my hope is to get into an art school and study there."

"You know getting an AA will help you get into art school. You could work and attend classes. Maybe find a flexible job so you can afford the right school."

I looked from Dad to Brittani in suspicion. They seemed to be sharing some secret I wasn't privy to.

Brittani smiled at me and I knew she was about to drop the bomb. "Sydney, your father and I have been talking, and well, we just don't get to see you very much, and when college starts next year, who knows how often we'll see you then."

Uh-huh. Like Brittani cared about spending time with me.

"So your father and I thought of a perfect solution," she said brightly, but her smile had a calculating quality.

"And what would that be?" I asked, trying not to blurt out, "Restore my college fund?" since that was *my* perfect solution.

"Brittani and I would like you to come live with us. When the baby is born. You could go to classes and get your education and spend time with your new sibling."

"You want me to live with you?" I repeated, trying to understand what he was offering me.

"Of course, and in exchange for room and board, we would ask that you care for your little brother or sister from time to time in between classes."

I looked at my father and then at Brittani. Both were beaming at the suggestion that I come live with them and be a free nanny while attending community college, which apparently, I would still be paying for myself instead of pursuing my dream of going to art school. This was my dad's perfect solution. It was perfect all right. Perfect for him.

"I don't think so, Dad," I said woodenly.

"What?" He seemed genuinely baffled.

I felt the anger boiling inside of me. "I'm sorry. Maybe I didn't make myself clear. Perhaps I should have put it this way. It will be a cold day in hell before I will ever live with you and be a free nanny for *her*."

I stood up, threw my napkin down on the plate, and stormed out of the restaurant, down the street, and around the corner. Tears streamed down my face and I could barely see. I slowed when the stitch in my side made it impossible to keep such a fast pace. I stopped and leaned against a brownstone, crying for what seemed like hours.

After I started to calm down, I fished out the map in my purse. Then I fought back tears again. I carried a map and never left the room without a fully charged cell phone. I kept emergency money in my shoe. I was a good girl. I was a good girl, and he still left us. And now he wanted me back as a servant to his new family.

I pulled out my phone and called my mom, but she wasn't home. I tried Katy next but got no answer. Finally I called Marlena. She answered on the second ring, like always, and said, "Sydney darling. What can I do for you?"

Not, "Sydney, why are you calling me?" or "What do you want from me?" but a caring "What can I do for you?" A torrent of words rushed out of my mouth and I told Marlena everything. I told her about lunch with my dad and his insidious offer. She didn't interrupt me. She didn't defend him. She didn't offer any psychological insight. She simply listened. And when I was spent, had shared all I could, she asked me where I was and promised to pick me up.

I managed to pull myself together by the time she arrived. She insisted we have tea inside the hotel in case I needed to talk some more, but there was really nothing else to tell.

"Sydney dear, tonight it's just you and me. What do you say? Just two crazy girls for a night on the town. Screw the red appointment. Nothing could be more boring than an art opening. Let me take you to the most divine club. Very exclusive. We'll let our hair down. No press and you can shake off this awful day. What do you say?"

"*You* are suggesting we blow off a red appointment? My, I must be pretty pathetic." I gave her a watery smile.

"You have had a simply wretched day, my darling. I must insist. You and I tonight. No silly art show or bodyguard nonsense. Just a night out for the girls. The Usurper be damned."

I laughed when she used my term for the new baby. It wasn't the little one's fault its parents totally sucked, but still, I couldn't quite embrace it yet, either.

"Okay then. I'm convinced. What should I wear?"

"Tonight you may wear whatever your heart desires. But keep in mind I'm not taking you to the ritziest area. I am partial to dives myself." She laughed and I joined her. Marlena's idea of a dive would be a place without valet parking.

"I'll pick you up at ten, darling," she said as she rose to leave.

I stayed at the table a while longer by myself. I wouldn't see Carl tonight. Maybe that was okay. How pathetic was I anyway? I'd turned into the poor relation and it wasn't something I wanted to brag about.

Tonight I was going to forget all about my dad and his new family. They wanted a nanny? I'd make them regret even *thinking* I was an appropriate role model for a child. Starting tonight.

SEVEN

I WAS READY TO GO. I HAD ON MY LOW-RISE jeans and the scarf top from Marlena and a pair of high-heeled shoes. I decided to use some of the tips and tricks I picked up from the makeup artists on shoots and was very happy with the results. Not too shabby. Smokey eyes without the heavily applied eyeliner, bee-stung lips, and translucent skin. A light dusting of glitter powder made me sparkle when I moved. I blew dry my hair straight so it partially covered my face and swung freely without tons of hair gel weighing it down.

Marlena took one look at me and whistled low. "You look magnificent, darling. The real Sydney Turner."

I didn't bother to correct her but returned the compliment

since she looked fabulous herself. The real Sydney Turner wore yoga pants that were too short and tank tops while sitting on a park bench sketching people. She clipped her hair out of her face and only wore lip gloss. That was the *real* Sydney Turner.

Tonight I was an NYC supermodel.

"Where are we going?" I asked once we were in the taxi.

"Soho," she told me, then gave the driver an address.

We arrived outside an ordinary looking club with a long line of people already waiting to get in. Instead of worrying, I let Marlena lead the way to the bouncer. They greeted each other with a hug and we walked past the line. Marlena knew absolutely everybody worth knowing. We made our way through the crowded club and right to the bar. Again we hit a line but Marlena received two lemon-drop martinis without having to order. She gave me one.

I took a sip and made a face. It was sour but the glass was laced with sugar so it wasn't unpleasant. Like lemonade with a kick.

"I have a weakness for drinks that taste like candy," Marlena confessed. We made rounds and I met so many people I couldn't begin to remember their names. I had no idea how many drinks I was served. I never paid for any of them, my glass was always full, and we were the center of attention all night. Marlena was the perfect party partner.

The techno beat had me swaying and before I knew it,

I was on the dance floor. I danced with everyone. I remembered no one. One minute I was dancing with a bunch of girls and the next I was grinding with some hot guy. I didn't care. It was like I was having an out-of-body experience. The real Sydney wasn't partying at a New York City hot spot. She was buried away watching the *supermodel* work the crowd.

It was well after two in the morning when I found myself in the arms of the most arresting guy. He'd been watching me all night. He matched my height and possessed a wiry strength. He said his name was Lucias, and I'd never seen bluer eyes on anyone in my life. He had sandy blond hair with a hint of stubble on his face, and he smelled of sandalwood and ocean. My two favorite scents.

"I've been anticipating this, Sydney," he murmured into my ear as he moved around me on the dance floor.

I laughed, though he wasn't being particularly funny. I wasn't the most graceful dancer but all the drinks made me feel like I was a superstar.

We circled again, hands skimming each others' shoulders and arms. I was barely aware of people staring at us, as our bodies moved in perfect unison. I had no idea who this Lucias was, but we matched rhythms, and our bodies seemed to mirror each other.

He trailed his hand up my back and cupped my neck firmly as he aligned his body with mine. My hand rested on his hip and the beat morphed into a techno salsa. Hip to hip, he masterfully led me through some complicated steps I didn't know. I'd never learned how to salsa but I was dancing like a pro with Lucias leading me. Our eyes locked, and he seemed to transmit every step variation to me through his body and stare. I couldn't look away. I never wanted the dance to end. I felt invincible, powerful, and superior to all the other people in the club.

Just Lucias and me.

My body gleamed with moisture but I didn't mind. Nothing mattered but dancing with Lucias. He was so attractive, so powerful, it reminded me of someone else. For a fleeting moment I thought of Carl but the image dissipated quickly and was replaced with a pair of sky blue eyes.

"Follow me," he said, and I nodded meekly. It was the most natural thing in the world to take his hand and follow him to the back of the club, out the door, and into the humid night.

Everything looked odd, like I was viewing it from a lens that was out of focus at the edges. My vision started to spin until Lucias turned and looked at me. His eyes. His magnificent blue eyes seemed to right the world.

I leaned forward into his embrace. He stood still, allowing my boldness. Our bodies touched and I was amazed at how cool he felt on such a hot night. I wanted to melt into him, he felt so refreshing. The thought frightened me for a moment and then the sensation passed.

It was the most natural thing in the world to want to

dissolve into Lucias. He was everything. I slipped my arms around his neck and pulled him toward me. It was so unlike me but I didn't care. I wanted this man to kiss me. I wanted to feel like we were one person. I needed to. His eyes commanded it. I had never wanted anything more in my life. Nothing else mattered. Not my parents, not Marlena and modeling, not Carl.

I hesitated a moment.

Carl.

I trembled when Lucias's lips moved toward mine. They were cool and firm, full and soft. The trembling increased when his tongue swept into my mouth. I clutched at his shoulders and felt myself drowning in his kisses. He embraced me, supported me, held me up. I couldn't stop shaking as his kisses trailed down my neck.

His lips felt cool and refreshing, like an ice cube melting down my hot skin. His tongue flicked out and I gasped in surprise. It felt like he bit me but that sensation quickly passed. Was he sucking on my neck? Giving me a hickey? I struggled, but only in my mind. My body still clutched him, pulling me closer. I closed my eyes and felt a tear slide down my face. Was I crying?

EIGHT

WAKING UP IN MY OWN BED AT THE RITZ WAS not what I expected. At all. Someone was rustling about and I tried to open my eyes. Light flooded the room, blinding me, and I groaned, squeezing my lids closed. I reached out with my arm, desperately searching for a pillow to put over my face to block the light.

"Ah, you're awake. Let me turn the lights down." I heard Marlena flip the switch, and I opened one eye experimentally.

"Better?" she asked.

"Much, thank you." I must have drank more than I realized to be so sensitive to light. Sitting up in the bed I made two monumental discoveries. One, I was wearing my nightgown and couldn't remember putting it on, and two, the side of my neck ached.

"How's the neck?" she asked as she tidied up around the desk where she was seated. What was she doing over there?

I ignored her neck question because it didn't seem relevant when *I was not wearing the clothes I went out in.* "Marlena, what happened to my clothes?"

"You wanted to sleep in those, did you?" She lifted a perfectly arched brow in question.

"No, but I wanted to remove them. Myself. Lucias didn't bring me home, did he?"

"Of course he did. You think I carried you all the way up here?"

"Marlena . . ." I whined and she laughed, taking pity on me.

"He may have carried you to bed, but I changed you into something more comfortable. That was your concern, right?"

I sighed in relief. I vaguely remembered dirty dancing with the sexy and exciting Lucias. There was even a recollection of getting fresh air in the back alley and a heated kiss or two. But Lucias wasn't Carl. I thought we went back afterward but things got blurry after that.

I couldn't remember the rest of last night. I suppose this was the reason Mom warned against drinking excessively. She just seemed to get smarter and smarter as I got older.

"Some party, huh?" Marlena dropped down on the bed next to me. "Wouldn't your father have had a fit?"

"Yeah, I'd say so. I'm so thirsty," I said.

"Thought you might be." She offered me a warm cup of something.

"What's this?" I eyed the dark liquid suspiciously.

"A little hair of the dog." Marlena smirked at me. "Come on, drink it before it spoils. It's fresh."

I sipped at it experimentally. The warm liquid tasted lovely. I took another sip and found myself emptying the entire glass. I felt deliciously satiated and energized.

"Wow, I feel great now. What was that?" I pulled the covers off and jumped up. I don't think I ever had such energy in the morning before.

"I call it '*Tasse de Marlena*.' "

It was better than my precious Dew. "I think I need a whole crate load of that stuff."

"Not likely," she said dryly, watching me bound around the room, grabbing clothes and heading into the bathroom.

I showered in record time. I wondered if I was still buzzed from the night before because my blood seemed to hum in my veins. I might have been partying all night but my skin had never looked better. It was flawless and my hair was shiny and styled exactly the way I like it. Everything seemed effortless, but I felt a little off. Sort of odd, like when I drew a cartoon with lots of frantic lines. I almost felt like

I would explode out of my skin at any moment. It was too weird.

I returned to the bedroom and asked Marlena, "There wasn't a little something extra in that drink was there?"

"Why, what ever do you mean?" she asked in mock innocence.

"You know, some sort of pick-me-up?" I hedged for a confirmation.

She leaned over and grabbed the TV remote, turned it on, and started flipping through channels. "Well, I do admit a need for a little pick-me-up once in a while but I swear it was clean. I haven't had so much as an aspirin since Soho, two nights ago."

"What are you talking about, Marlena? Are you saying I've been passed out for two days?"

She clicked over to CNN and showed me the date stamp on the screen. It was Monday night.

"But, but, I had to work today! Didn't I?" I tried to fight off that feeling of exploding at the seams again.

"I canceled the shoot." Marlena sounded so blasé. She was the one who color coded the appointments in the first place. What was going on? "I brought over your new schedule. Over there on the desk."

I glanced at the schedule. They were all night shoots and "things." They were all in blue and red. No more green appointments.

"Marlena, these are all at night. When am I going to sleep?"

She sighed heavily and looked at me. "Of course they're all at night. Did you think you could hang out in the sun without burning to a crisp? Really, Sydney, think about it. Vampires can't go out in the sun."

Oh. My. God.

"Don't look at me like that. Who do you think Lucias was, anyway? Just another hot guy? Wasn't he captivating? Didn't it all seem like a dream you couldn't control? When he took you outside, did he kiss you?" She sounded almost jealous. "Did he hold you tight and give you a little love bite?"

My mind spun. The dancing with Lucias. My trancelike state and doing all those things that were so unlike me.

I grabbed at the side of my neck, rushed into the bathroom for the mirror, and searched for a cut, teeth marks, something. If I stared hard enough I could see two puncture marks. They looked more like scars than fresh wounds. Even when I poked at them, they were barely tender. The earlier ache was gone.

I gripped the edge of the counter with my hands and squeezed my eyes shut. I was losing control. Part of me was slipping away and I couldn't hold on to it, no matter what.

I felt the vanity give before I heard it crack. I let go quickly. It clung precariously to the wall, the pipes straining to keep it intact.

Marlena was instantly behind me, surveying the damage. "Sydney! You have to be careful! You have super strength now. How am I going to explain this to the hotel?" She snapped her fingers. "I've got it! I'll leak to the press you had a party and broke the vanity having sex on it with, hmmm, who should we link you to now? Maybe that actor from your first 'thing,' what was his name again?"

I grabbed her shoulders and demanded, "What are you saying? What's happening to me?"

She cried out in pain and I immediately released her. Her eyes widened with fear, and she cringed when I tried to pat her shoulder in apology.

"I'm so sorry, Marlena. I didn't mean to hurt you. I just don't know what's going on. Please, don't look at me like that."

She was breathing heavily, and I smelled her uncertainty. It excited me, and part of me wanted to reach out again and see what she'd do. Would she scream? Would she struggle to escape?

The humming in my veins got louder.

I rushed past her to the opposite side of the room. We needed distance.

She tentatively peeked out from the bathroom. "I know this is overwhelming, Syd," she said hesitantly. When I didn't fly toward her in a fit of rage, she grew more confident. "Just think about what this means. You're a good model.

Now, with your new, ah, attributes, you'll be even better on film. Yes, I know you probably thought vampires couldn't see their own reflections or be photographed but that's an old wives' tale." She chuckled nervously.

"Are you . . ."—I couldn't bring myself to say the word—"one, too?"

For a moment she looked very sad, but it passed quickly so I couldn't be sure. "Of course not. You've seen me during the day. At the airport? At daytime shoots? Lunch with your dad? No, I'm just a humble servant of Vamp Modeling Inc. Not all are worthy enough to be considered for the change, Sydney. I had to fight for you. The boss didn't think you'd be such a natural."

My mouth opened but no sound came out. She fought for me to become like this?

"Now, it's true you can't go out in the sun and you'll need to adjust to a new, uh, diet, but look at all the advantages. You can work forever. Be beautiful and young *forever*." She sighed wistfully, and I saw the longing on her face from across the room.

"And, darling, you have the power to mesmerize anyone and bend them to your will! They'll believe anything you tell them. You could rob a bank and make someone else confess to the crime." She giggled at her joke but stopped when I didn't join in. "Sydney, you can have your father back. Isn't that what you always wanted?"

I rallied from my numbness at that statement. "But what about Brittani?"

Marlena, more confident now, strolled over to me and gathered my hands in hers. "Dearest Syd, you can make it so there is no Brittani."

"The baby?" I whispered.

"You can be free of the Usurper for once and all. Just do what's in your nature. Feed and make Brittani believe she did it. . . ."

I looked at Marlena in horror. How could she even suggest such a thing? And the worse part, the very deepest, ugliest truth in my soul, was that I was tempted.

Britanni robbed me of my entire family life—she deserved to be punished. Dad owed me his love and loyalty. Mom deserved that condo on the water, and I felt the seams that had held me together start to unravel.

"Vamp Modeling Inc. can help you in so many ways, Sydney," Marlena continued. "We'll schedule all of your work at night. We can help you adjust to this new existence. You'll be free. Freer than you ever imagined, with all the power you deserve."

Her eyes glittered in the dark room and I saw what lay in her heart. I wanted to scream.

"You did this to me," I whispered in shock. "It was you."

"Of course, darling. Without me you'd still be crying

over losing your daddy's love. He doesn't deserve you! I made you young and beautiful forever. I made you a goddess! It's my gift to you, Sydney. Vamp Modeling's gift to you. You and I will continue to take the modeling world by storm. There will be no limit to your potential."

"I trusted you. You were my friend!" I grabbed her wrists and pulled her forward.

She winced but didn't back down. "You're not a child any longer, Sydney. I helped you, didn't I? I came up with the plan to embarrass your father, just like you wanted. I made you a household name and the star of the tabloids and Page Six. I made you! I gave you immortality! You owe me now."

I released her wrists abruptly, shocked by her change in countenance.

She advanced on me, spewing her truth like poison.

"You're not in Seattle now. How do you think Daddy will react when he discovers his daughter is undead? Do you think that offer to live with him will still stand? Do you think they'll let you anywhere near them?

"And what about your mom? Imagine the look in her eyes when your stomach growls and she sees the hunger in you? Do you think she'll embrace you with open arms then? Oh, I think not, Sydney. You're ours now. You belong to Vamp Modeling Inc. We own you."

Marlena swept past me, jerked open the door, and turned

back, as though nothing had just happened between us. "Don't forget about your shoot tomorrow at 10:00 P.M. dear. If we get done at a decent hour, there's a "thing" to attend afterward. Ciao."

The door shut and I sank to my knees on the plush carpet.

NINE

LAYING FETAL ON THE FLOOR TOOK UP MOST OF my evening, but even I had to stop the pity party sometime. At first I thought Marlena was just crazy. And she was crazy, clearly. But she'd sucked me into her little fantasy world and changed my life forever. All under the guise of "helping me." I shivered remembering the look in her eyes. No soul. It was terrifying to witness.

Where did all this leave me? She was right about my dad. I couldn't tell him. And my mom? Even if she believed me, she certainly wouldn't want a blood-sucking daughter.

Blood sucking.

I scrambled to the cup Marlena gave me earlier and looked at the residue. It was red. I checked the garbage can.

There was a rubber hose like they use when you give blood and a needle connected to a syringe. She must have drained her own blood into a cup, anticipating my thirst when I awoke.

I was going to be sick.

I rushed to the bathroom and leaned over the porcelain. My mind demanded I puke up the blood but my body refused. It wanted the blood, needed it. And refused to give it up. Worst of all, I knew I'd want it again.

The phone rang. *Who would be calling me at this hour?* I was afraid to pick it up. Afraid it would be Marlena.

It rang again and I grabbed the handle, just so I wouldn't have to hear the startling noise. *Did the phones always sound so loud?*

"Hello?"

"Hey, Syd. Did I wake you up?" Carl sounded almost hopeful.

"Uh no, no. I was awake. Are you here to pick me up?" I was confused. I just couldn't do a "thing" tonight. I couldn't.

"No. I was, uh, I heard you went out with Marlena the other night, and I thought I'd check and see how you were doing."

He sounded concerned and shy at the same time. I gripped the phone tighter, struggling with what to say.

"Yeah, I had a fight with my dad so Marlena thought a girls' night out would help." My voice broke on the last word, but I cleared my throat and continued. "It was this club in Soho I hadn't been to before." *And I'll never go to again.*

"Was it the Silent Scream?" he asked nervously.

I remembered two *S*'s with a picture of a screaming zombie on the napkins. "Yeah, I think so."

Carl was quiet a moment, as though soaking in this new information. He finally asked, "How'd it go?"

My veins hummed and I tried to hold back the feeling of panic and loss of control. I felt like I was standing on the edge of a cliff and my whole body was begging to jump off into the night air. I knew if I jumped I would be lost forever.

But I couldn't tell Carl that. "Oh you know. Same ol', same ol'. It took my mind off my dad." *That was the understatement of the year.*

"Are you sure you're okay?" Carl sounded like he needed reassurance. But I couldn't cope with anything else right now.

"Fine. Never been better. So I'll see you tomorrow night, right?"

"Sure, tomorrow at ten." I was about to hang up when he added, "You know, you can tell me anything, Syd. I'm here for you."

I should have called Carl instead of Marlena after the fight with my dad. But it was too late. There was nothing Carl could do for me now.

"Thanks." I choked on the words as I hung up.

It was the middle of the night but I was wide awake. The

newly awakened devil on my shoulder goaded my inner angel to check out the town with my new senses. I wanted to go to Central Park and walk in the night air and feel the energy of the city around me. It was exciting and terrifying all at once.

I finally talked myself into it. I wasn't some sociopathic killer. I was a vampire. I never knew they really existed until now so they must be pretty low key. Surely they weren't out there sucking people dry or they would have been discovered.

So I felt pretty safe. I crept down the hallway to the elevators but opted for the stairs, which was crazy considering what floor I was on. But I raced down the stairs with amazing speed and arrived at the lobby in no time. I felt invincible, exuberant, and jubilant. It was like my body was meant to run.

Crossing the lobby, I shielded my eyes from the bright opalescence of the chandeliers and made my way to the front door. One of the doormen held the door and asked, "Do you need a taxi, Ms. Turner?"

"No, I'm good," I said and stared at the pulse in his temple. It seemed to jump out at me.

He smiled in sort of a goofy way. "Can I get you anything else? Anything at all?"

I jerked my eyes away from his temple and looked at him. He was middle-aged, married. And he was looking at me like a love-starved teenager.

I shook my head and moved away as he stared at me intently. How easy it would be to lead him away from his post and taste the delicious nectar of his blood. Feel him shudder in my arms. I quickened my pace toward Central Park. Afraid if I slowed, I would easily turn around and do the treacherous things my body wanted.

I entered the park from the south. It was deserted for the most part. During the day it was filled with kids, the elderly, and everyone in between, enjoying the weather in the beautiful natural setting. I strolled along the paths between flowering trees and into the shadows. It was crazy to hang out in the park alone at night. My mother would have a heart attack if she knew what I was doing. But I needed to be out.

I felt invincible.

I sensed my prey long before I actually saw them. Two men followed me along the tree-lined path. Ridiculous really. They were so loud. I could smell them. I stilled and inhaled deeply. The hum in my veins quickened. Every pore in my body tingled with excitement. The hunt was on.

I dropped to one knee and pretended to tie my laces. As I predicted, they took this moment to catch up to me.

"Give me your money," the shorter of the two demanded, flashing a switchblade. At least I thought it was a switchblade but I'd never been mugged before so I couldn't be entirely sure.

The other looked around nervously, his head twitching. He smelled sour. *Drugs,* I guessed.

I put my hands up and warned, "Don't you know how dangerous it is to be out this late at night?"

"Shut up, bitch! And give me your money or I'll cut you!"

Well, that was just rude. I slowly reached into my pocket and pulled out a few loose bills I'd tucked there. When he darted forward to grab the cash, I swiftly caught hold of the hand that held the blade. He appeared, to me, to move as though in slow motion. I squeezed his wrist just a little and felt it pop. He screamed. I released him just as his other hand, balled in a fist, came at me. I blocked it easily with my forearm and grabbed him by the throat.

I smelled his fear now as he gasped for breath. I lifted him just enough that his feet barely touched the pathway. His friend stood frozen, like a deer in the headlights.

"Shhhhh," I whispered to my victim, careful not to crush his windpipe. He gurgled and struggled but couldn't get away. His uninjured hand was clutched at his neck.

I took my time looking at his dirty face. Almost lovingly I trailed a finger down his cheek. Cocking my head to one side I shook it in disappointment. "I warned you it was dangerous here at night," I reminded him in a lover's whisper. The humming in my veins filled me with an ecstasy I'd never known before. It was so easy. He was so fragile, so weak. He was mine to toy with, to drink from, to discard.

I smiled, aware that my fangs had come out. The man blanched and renewed his struggle to escape. I turned his neck so I could see the life-giving vein pulsing through his terrified system. One small twist and I could snap his neck. But it would be all over and I didn't want it to be over. I wanted to taste the adrenaline in his blood.

Almost savagely, I bit him. I knew I could numb his neck with my saliva, as Lucias had done for me, but I didn't want to ease his fear, I wanted to inflame it. His blood filled my mouth and I drank deeply. It was sweet. Much sweeter than Marlena's had been. It was the fear, I knew. The fear made it all that much sweeter.

I knew I could drain him. I could drink it all and discard him like he was nothing, though my brain screamed for me to stop. I might have continued if his pal hadn't screamed. I pulled away in time to see him sprint off into the trees. When I looked back at the face in front of me, I saw terror, tears, and the knowledge of the inevitable etched across his features. He knew he was going to die. That I was going to kill him.

Gently, almost tenderly, I put him down, but his legs refused to hold him. I supported him as he collapsed to the dusty trail. I tentatively licked his wounds, instantly healing them. I stroked his head like my mother used to comfort me and hummed a tuneless lullaby.

"Shhh, don't cry," I crooned. "It's gonna be okay. I won't hurt you anymore. I promise."

His eyes were still wide with fear. He didn't believe me, of course. And who could blame him. I'd just savagely drank his blood; a little nicety now wasn't going to make him forget that. So I looked into his gray eyes and held the stare. I felt his internal struggle. He didn't want to look at me. He wanted to close his eyes and curl up into a ball and hide but he wouldn't. He would stare at me as long as I commanded it.

I told him to seek help for his arm and to forget what happened here. Then I stood up and walked away.

TEN

I WENT BACK TO MY ROOM AND TRIED, IN VAIN, to block out what I'd done. I'd liked scaring that man. I enjoyed seeing his terror. It didn't matter that I made him forget afterward. The look on his face would haunt me. I couldn't believe what I'd become and I had nowhere to turn. What was I going to do?

Around dawn I fell asleep. The sound of the telephone woke me. "Hello?" I answered groggily.

"Taking a little nap are we?" Carl's warm voice filled me with pleasure.

The clock said 9:30 . . . P.M. "Oh no, I overslept!" I jumped to my feet, looking frantically for something to wear.

"Well, technically I'm a little early," he admitted.

"Ah, well then I feel so much better," I replied sarcastically as I ransacked drawers for something to wear. "What's the weather like?" I pulled out a pair of shorts.

"Hot and muggy. Like everyday. What are you doing?"

I grunted with the effort of pulling on my shorts and holding the phone. "Getting dressed," I answered, nearly falling over in my haste to find a tank top.

"So you mean to tell me you weren't dressed one second ago?"

"Aha!" I said triumphantly as I pulled the shirt successfully over my head. "Dressed in record time."

"Tease," he murmured. I could imagine him shaking his head in mock dismay.

I laughed and told him I'd be down in a minute. I rushed to brush my teeth and was surprised to discover I looked great. I didn't look tired and puffy from too much sleep. My skin glowed, my hair fell into place perfectly, and my eyes had never looked more clear or green.

Then the memories of last night flooded over me. I remembered what I was. I was no longer a girl rushing to a modeling shoot. I was a *vampire* going to work for Vamp Modeling Inc., which now owned me. It took the lift out of my step.

I met Carl downstairs. I was feeling sorry for myself by then so when he said, "You look—"

I finished his sentiment by supplying, "Beautiful? Young?

Ethereal? Perfect?" Each word was said with more sarcasm than the last.

He put his hands up in surrender. "I was going to say you look like you have something on your mind."

I flushed with shame. It wasn't Carl's fault I was in this mess. I opened the back door—to his surprise—and climbed in. I mumbled a lame, "Sorry," and looked out the window as he took the driver's seat with a puzzled expression on his face. I didn't trust myself to ride shotgun. To be so close to him. What if I got hungry and tried to feed on him? I couldn't bear the look of terror and fear in his eyes. The look of betrayal.

At the shoot Marlena greeted me like always, like nothing was out of the ordinary. What a total whack job.

I went to hair and makeup like a zombie. I was modeling Fendi handbags today. Wouldn't Katy be thrilled? The thought of Katy brought tears to my eyes. How could I tell her what happened to me? She'd never be my friend now. She couldn't even watch scary movies without sleeping with the light on. A vampire as a best friend? Or, better yet, a vampire who got off on scaring her prey? No, she would never be my friend now.

It's not easy to sell "happy" when you're miserable. After several unsuccessful attempts to cajole me into a playful mood, the photographer called for a recess and had a private word with Marlena. *Great, now I was going to get yelled at.* I didn't think I could handle another Marlena scene.

"Sydney darling, let's take a walk shall we?" she suggested as the crew buzzed around us to set up the next shot. I dutifully joined her and we strolled around the huge loft, arm in arm.

"I know this will take some getting used to," Marlena empathized. "But, darling, you've got to snap out of it. Claude wants a happy model and you're giving him, well, a sad model pretending to be happy. And not pretending very well, may I add." She smiled at her own joke and squeezed my arm in reassurance.

My stomach growled, which Marlena believed was causing my sadness. "Why, darling, no wonder you're so off. You haven't fed yet? Dear me, this won't do. Let's get you a nice cuppa cuppa."

"No!" I said a little too forcefully. "I totally, uh, ate before the shoot. That was just me digesting. I got some news from home is all. I missed Katy's big birthday bash. She turned eighteen without me."

Marlena eyed me suspiciously but then nodded. "Of course, it's hard to be away from home. You've been gone a good two months without seeing your friends. That must be hard. I tell you what. We'll have a big birthday bash for you. We'll invite everyone!"

She clapped her hands together in delight and steered me off toward the shoot, satisfied she'd solved all my problems and I would be happy again.

I did end up giving the photographer happy, but only

after he promised I would get my pick of Fendi bags if I could smile pretty. I thought of how happy Katy would be when I gave her a new Fendi bag and the Ferragamo sunglasses. I just needed Lohan's autograph. It might not make up for losing a best friend who was a vampire, but it would be a nice consolation package.

The shoot ended and it was time for a "thing." I officially hated "things" now. At one time they were exciting but now I knew I would be fighting my instincts to feed on people all night. I played the scenario out in my head.

"Have you met such and such?"

"Oh yes, I loved you on *The O.C.* Could I see you in the alleyway for a little cuppa cuppa?"

Can you just imagine?

So I spent the next couple of weeks avoiding everyone at the "things." Marlena was not thrilled with my lack of bad girl behavior but she couldn't make me be a bad girl if I didn't want to. She still tried to get the press to do the wild child angle but they were losing interest in me.

The shoots were a similar problem. I wasn't happy. What happened to the beautiful young girl who laughed into the camera? Where was that inner vibrancy now? Sure, I still photographed well but that inner light they loved was now missing and it worried Marlena.

"Dear, the powers-that-be are not happy," she stated after a particularly nonclimactic shoot.

"What do you mean?" I asked warily.

"Your contract is almost up and we aren't getting the job requests we hoped for. They say something is missing."

"You mean like my soul?" I retorted sarcastically.

"Don't be ridiculous," she said sharply. "You still have your soul. It's just missing a piece is all."

Oddly her claim made me feel better. I wasn't some soulless monster. I was just lacking. Surely I wasn't totally lost if I still had most of my soul, right?

"What are you saying, Marlena?"

She sighed dramatically. "I'm saying that they don't want to renew your modeling contract."

I stared at her in disbelief. Those bastards had me turned into a vampire so I could work for them forever and now they *changed their mind*? What did that mean for me?

"Are you freakin' kidding me?" I exclaimed.

"Yes, dear, I'm just as upset as you are about this whole thing." She tried to pat my arm reassuringly.

"No, I don't think you are, Marlena. I'm freakin' undead because of them and now they don't want me anymore? What am I going to do?"

She nodded her head in agreement. "I know, it simply isn't done. They have responsibilities. I'm doing my best, dear, I really am. I just wanted to prepare you for the worst, if it comes to that."

I didn't know what to say. What could be worse than being a vampire? Being an unemployed one? I couldn't believe this was happening to me.

"Now let's not dwell on it tonight. It's your special night, dear. Everyone will be at your birthday bash. Carl is taking you to the Silent Scream—you remember that place, right? Lucias and all his friends will be there, as well as your modeling friends. It will be so much fun."

I just stared at her with an open mouth. She was taking me back to the place where I was turned into a vampire for my eighteenth birthday. This was supposed to make me happy?

I practically ran to Carl's car after my conversation with Marlena. What was I going to do? All I ever wanted was college money to go to art school. I just wanted my dad to pay for what he did to Mom and me with a little fatherly humiliation. There was no way I could go home now. What if I woke up with hunger pains? No one was safe around me.

I was avoiding everyone I cared about in fear I would feed on them. Poor Carl probably thought he did something wrong because I wouldn't sit next to him. I barely spoke to him. Basically I kept as far away from him as I could.

And then there was the feeding. I waited until I was practically starving before I would feed and then I cried afterward because I always let the predator take over for the taste of fear in his blood.

Carl refrained from making any comment when I threw myself into the backseat. We drove to Soho and he kept looking at me through the rearview mirror. Finally I couldn't take it any longer. "What?" I demanded.

"You know, we don't have to go to this place tonight." He measured his words carefully.

I shook my head in despair. There was no way out. I turned to look out the window at all the lights and Carl didn't speak to me again.

When we arrived, I'd managed to pull myself together to some small degree. It was my birthday party. My last big hurrah before exile from the modeling world and the life I knew before. I should have fun and enjoy it. Even though my world was coming apart at the seams, I should try to have this one moment in time.

My stomach growled as Carl opened the door for me and I bit my lip in fear. I hadn't fed this evening. Maybe I could hold out long enough to make a quick trip to Central Park after the party. Could I last that long?

I arrived to cheers from people I didn't even know. Marlena called for the music to stop so she could announce my arrival.

"Friends, we are all here to honor our very own Sydney Turner on her eighteenth birthday." The crush of people hooted and hollered making Marlena pause before she continued, "This summer has been a sort of dream for me. I've grown so much knowing Sydney. She is like a gift herself. So join me as I raise a glass to her, on today, her eighteenth birthday!"

The crowd erupted with, "Hear, hear," and before I knew it, I was swept onto the dance floor. I saw other models I worked with before, up-and-coming actors, starlets, a few heirs to million-dollar fortunes, and some genuine stars. The music pounded and everyone was wishing me a happy birthday. Tonight would be perfect. If it wasn't for the fact that every face and body reminded me of my hunger. I could smell them all; see the pulses in their throats beat strong and quick.

A well-built arm pulled me into his embrace. Lucias smiled at me. His blue eyes were as clear as I remembered them, but they didn't hold the mesmerizing appeal they once had.

"Happy birthday, Sydney." He smiled, flashing his perfect teeth. We danced in perfect unison, our bodies remembering how well they matched one another.

Suddenly the air seemed to charge with electricity when Carl surprised me by cutting in and sweeping me away from Lucias. He was amazingly light on his feet and our bodies molded together as the beat slowed down.

"My savior," I joked without humor and Carl smirked in response.

"So you're speaking to me again, are you?" he questioned, maneuvering me like an expert across the floor.

I winced at the hurt tone in his voice. "I'm sorry, Carl. I've been going through things these last few weeks. Things I can't explain. Just know it has nothing to do with you. I still think you're, well, amazing." I looked up into his amber eyes and sighed the last word.

And he *was* amazing. He felt so strong and right, holding me. Carl made me feel safe. Like I could let him take care of all the ugliness that plagued me and he would make it better. For a moment, I pretended it was real. I closed my eyes and laid my head on his shoulder and just let his body move mine. It seemed like an eternity later when my stomach growled again. Slowly I turned my head and looked into his eyes.

I boldly lifted my lips to his. They were cool and firm. He seemed surprised by my daring in the middle of the dance floor, with a room full of people. But it was my birthday and I deserved a birthday kiss from Carl. I waited a whole summer for this moment and I wanted to know what it felt like.

Following quickly was that old familiar hum in my veins and I broke our kiss. His eyes were heavily lidded and he pulled me closer for more. I wanted it so badly but the hum was overpowering. I had to get away before I did something terribly wrong.

I pulled away and rushed off the dance floor. Of course, he followed.

"Get away from me!" I begged, pushing past the crowds of people in the club. I didn't know where to go. I just knew I was going to do something desperate if I didn't escape him.

I swallowed a sob as I reached the back door and threw

my weight into it. It practically collapsed under my strength, swinging out and slamming into the brick wall. Powdered masonry hung in the humid air as I looked around desperately. Surely there was someone I could grab. Anyone to feed from instead of Carl.

The alley was still, the air heavy with moisture. Carl pounded through the door, mere steps from me.

"What the hell, Sydney?" He was confused and angry. I could hardly blame him. I was warm and willing in his arms one minute and screaming to get away the next. He must think I'm crazy and he wouldn't be far off base because I felt like I was going insane.

"Please, Carl, stay away from me." I held out my hands as though to ward him off. I hoped my eyes would convey the depths of my intention but I knew they would sing the siren song of seduction. Vampires used their mesmerizing gaze to trap their victims, seduce them into compliance. My head might be screaming for Carl to run to safety, but my body, the animal I had become, wanted this prey.

I whimpered as he took a step closer. "Please, no. Go away." I moaned the final warning, backed up against the wall when his chest came in contact with my splayed hands. Instead of pushing him away, my fingers curled into fists full of his shirt and brought him closer.

I felt my whole body buzz with the excitement of victory when Carl drew closer.

"Leave me," I softly begged one last time but I knew it

was too late. I was standing on the edge of the precipice once again, the darkness calling to me. If I do this, I thought, if I feed from this man then I will have crossed over for sure. There will be nothing keeping me from falling into the eternal darkness. I sobbed once more as I pulled his lips down to mine.

"I'm so sorry," I mouthed as my lips touched his, capturing him so completely. I knew he was mine for the taking and when his arms wrapped around me, crushing me to his body, his tongue swept into my mouth and I clutched his shirt tighter.

You are *mine*, I thought savagely, kissing him harder. *You cannot escape me,* was my final coherent thought when I bit his lip and tasted blood. Trembling, I sucked to relish the salty goodness. He tasted so rich, so wonderful. Never had I tasted anything so refreshing. I needed him.

I gasped in surprise when he broke our kiss, grabbing my face between his hands and looked at me. I knew my eyes were red with need and the fangs I desperately wanted to deny were a part of me had come out. He didn't push me away or show his disgust. He locked his gaze with mine and I saw understanding reflected there.

He slowly brought my mouth to the side of his neck with its beautiful pulsing vein and offered himself up to me, like a willing sweet sacrifice. I wept as my fangs pierced his cool skin and I drank. I gulped with a vengeful thirst and clutched at his shoulders as I imbibed his blood.

I am lost, I thought dizzily. *Lost forever.* Truly I'd never known blood could be this fulfilling, this rich. There was no fear but his blood was sweeter than any I had before him. When I finished, I licked the wound slowly, feeling it heal beneath my tongue.

What had I done?

I looked up slowly, feeling him still tense beneath my hands. Would his eyes reflect terror before I made him forget? I almost couldn't bear to look at him but knew I must. I owed it to him. It was my penance to see the shock and betrayal in his once passionate eyes, directed at me. He trusted me and I'd broken that trust.

I lifted my face toward his and opened my eyes when I knew I could see into his. I gasped in shock at what I saw there. His eyes were aglow with scarlet need. His beautiful white smile flashed in the night, exposing two razor sharp fangs.

"My turn," he said simply and lowered his head to my neck. He was the hunter now and I his captive prey. I shuddered when I felt his fangs penetrate me, my blood flowing into him and my knees buckled. I was his, body and soul. There was no other way to describe it. He wasn't just feeding on me, he possessed me. Pulling me from the darkness and back to the light. He was saving me and I gripped him tighter. After long moments, I felt his tongue lovingly sweep across my neck.

My mind swirled with questions. "How? When?"

"Not here," he replied and took my hand in his. He led me around the alley, back down the street toward where he parked the car. It was quiet and muggy but my thoughts were a jumble of questions. Carl was a vampire. How did I not notice this before? Was I so wrapped up in my own problems I couldn't even sense another vampire?

He opened the door to the Town Car and I slid in. When he joined me behind the wheel I suddenly felt shy and awkward. Where did we start?

Carl began. "I was born in a small village in the mountains of Spain during the rule of General Franco. When I was fourteen, I was arrested and sent to jail in a labor camp. Five years passed and a group of us escaped the prison. I was the only one to survive.

"When I returned to my village, it had been burned to the ground. I was starved, exhausted, and barely alive when I was set upon by"—he paused a moment, as though the retelling were difficult despite his emotionless tone—"vampires. They changed me. I parted ways with them shortly thereafter and fled Spain."

"So you're Spanish?" I asked.

"No, I am Euskaldunak." I must have looked terribly confused because he clarified, "More commonly known as Basque." He smiled softly and the tension that was building during his tale started to ebb.

"What about your family?" I whispered. I really wished I paid more attention during history class

"Dead. They're all dead." I put my hand on his and he turned his palm up to caress it. "It's okay, Sydney. It was a long time ago. Before you were even born."

"That doesn't make it suck any less," I said defensively and he chuckled.

"I think it's your turn," he prompted.

"Well, I'm afraid after your story, mine is a little anticlimatic. About a month ago, after that big fight with my dad?" I looked at him and he nodded in memory. "Marlena took me here and I met a guy who, who"—I struggled with saying the words—"changed me."

"Why?" he asked and I looked at him like he was crazy.

"Why? You think I signed up for this? Marlena totally set me up. She wanted me to become some supermodel deity and convinced the powers-that-be at Vamp Modeling Inc. that I was the next Heidi Klum. Now they don't want to renew my contract. They say I've lost that vitality from my earlier work and I'm stuck and don't know what to do 'cause I can't go home and I can't stay here." I ended my tirade in a wail and started crying. Carl gathered me in his arms and I continued.

"When I get hungry I can't seem to control my need to feed and I'm afraid I might, I might . . ." I hiccupped, unable to continue.

He stroked my hair and kissed the top of my head, all the while murmuring some nonsense words I didn't recognize. It had a soothing effect and I managed to calm down.

"So now I'm totally screwed and don't know what I'm going to do. Maybe I could learn to drive a car in New York and do what you do?" I said hopefully, but I shuddered at the thought of manipulating New York traffic.

"So you didn't agree to this, uh, alternative lifestyle?" he clarified with a slight smile.

"Well, duh," I retorted.

"And would you be willing to make a formal statement to that effect?"

"What? To the police? Right, I'll just walk on into the local precinct and press charges against Vamp Modeling Inc. for unlawful vampire conversion," I scoffed at him.

He nodded his head vigorously. "That's exactly right, well, except the local police part. Sydney, what Marlena and Vamp Modeling Inc. have done is illegal in undead society. They cannot change a person into a vampire without prior consent and certainly not without a license."

"Illegal?" I echoed stupidly.

"Yes, as in against the law. Syd, I'm not really a bodyguard and driver. I'm a Vampire Investigator for the Tribunal, a government body of vampires. It's my job to investigate illegal vampire conversions. I'm on loan to the New York sector because of all the trouble they've been having with rogue vampires lately."

"You're a vampire cop?"

He chuckled at my expression, which was probably priceless.

"More or less."

"But what about me?"

"If you help us by pressing charges, then I can get you into a vampire acclimation program. You don't have to live out your undead existence alone, Sydney. There are thousands of us."

"But what about the, uh, *feeding*? I don't want to do that anymore, Carl! I don't like who I become when I'm hungry!"

He nodded in understanding. "Sydney, being a vampire takes getting used to. You are a predator now. It's important to accept what you've become, even if it was against your will. However there are ways to deal with the changes. I imagine you wait until you are starving before you feed, right?"

I nodded.

"But by then, the chase gets very exciting and you know the blood will be sweeter and you hate how you toy with someone before you feed, even if you make them forget it afterward?"

My eyes opened wide. *Yes, that was exactly it. How did he know?*

"Sydney, every new vampire goes through that. It's not uncommon at all. The trick is to feed before you're starving.

Then you're not tempted to scare or chase someone because you're in a feeding frenzy. All of this information should have been available to you after the change. That's why we require licenses now."

"Really?" I asked hopefully. Could I really make it through this mess?

"Yes, really." He stroked my hair again and I rested my head on his shoulder. After a moment, I said, "What do you need me to do?"

ELEVEN

CARL TOOK ME TO THE VAMPIRE AUTHORITIES. I filled out a ton of paperwork and made my statement to a very sweet looking girl, who couldn't be more than fifteen years old. After I was through, Carl drove me back to the Ritz.

"Will I have to come back here for a trial or anything?" I asked almost hopefully, so I could see Carl again.

"No, now that we have your statement, everything is set. They've been investigating this company for a while now."

"What will happen to Marlena?" I knew I shouldn't care, after all she did to me, but Marlena was the closest thing to a friend I had in New York, even if she did think I should be a vampire.

"Marlena is a registered servant of the undead. She won't get off lightly. She'll probably have her status revoked and have to leave Vamp Modeling Inc."

I shivered. Marlena loved her job. And I believed she held out hope she could someday be a vampire. She'd lost her dream for good now.

"What do I do?" I asked uncertainly.

"You get to go home. They have you booked on a flight for tomorrow night."

"Oh," I said, surprised. He held out a file folder bursting with paperwork.

"This is information you should have been given before the change. Read it and I'll pick you up tomorrow night to take you to the airport."

I nodded numbly and slid toward the door. Carl touched my shoulder and I looked up at him.

"Do you trust me, Sydney?" I stared into his handsome face. After all I'd been through, it was funny. I did trust Carl. Carl made me feel safe.

I nodded to him before leaving the car and made my way back to my room. I sent e-mail to my mom and Katy, explaining I would be coming home a few days early. I kept the messages brief because I really didn't know how much to tell them. And then I read the packet of information Carl gave me.

It was amazing. There were websites with special vampire log-ins. Mixers and socials for new vampires in the Seattle area, community events and so much more. I started to feel better. There was even a vampire-friendly university and I was surprised to discover they had a much-respected art program. I fell asleep reading.

I woke up in time to pack all my stuff, carrying the Fendi bag and Ferragamo sunglasses. I never did get Lindsay Lohan's autograph. I guess two out of three wasn't bad. The phone rang and I knew Carl was here.

I didn't want to think about how I wouldn't be seeing him again after this. It didn't seem fair that the one guy I felt I could connect with *and* who would accept my vampire status lived across the country from me.

Carl met me in the lobby and carried my stuff out to the Town Car. I was confused but didn't know what to say when another driver took my things from Carl and put them in the trunk. Carl joined me in the backseat.

"I don't understand. Who is this guy? Aren't you driving me to the airport?" I was happy Carl was sitting with me, but I didn't want some stranger listening to our conversation the whole way there.

"This guy is Mark, and don't worry, he's a vampire. You can talk freely in front of him and I *am* taking you to the airport." He slipped his hand into mine like it was the most natural thing in the world.

"Well obviously, since you are sitting next to me but why aren't you driving?" I questioned.

"Dying to get rid of me, is that it?" he teased and I gripped his hand tighter.

"You know I'm not."

"Nervous?" he asked and I nodded. I still didn't know why he wasn't driving but I'd let him keep his secret for now. So many things ran through my head. What would I say to my mom? What about Katy?

Carl reached inside a bag next to him and pulled out a DVD case.

"I almost forgot. I got you this."

Puzzled, I took the case and gasped. It was a copy of *Mean Girls* and it was signed by Lindsay Lohan.

"When? How did you get this?" He laughed at my excitement.

"I got it from Ms. Lohan at your birthday party. She was there. Didn't you see her?"

I tried to remember everyone I saw but just couldn't. I was so hungry that night and was only concentrating on not feeding on Carl. I can't believe I didn't notice freakin' Lindsay Lohan at my party.

"So you carry a copy of *Mean Girls* with you, just in case?" I teased, turning it over in my hands.

"That, or there was a video store a block from the club."

"Katy is gonna be thrilled," I said. "Thank you." And I leaned over and kissed him on the lips.

"I can't wait to meet Katy and your mom," he answered against my lips.

I pulled back in shock. "What? You're coming with me?"

Carl laughed. "Did you think I was taking you to the airport and letting you face your family and friend alone? Sydney, I live in Seattle. I told you I was on loan to New York but I am actually based out of Seattle."

I couldn't believe it. Carl was coming home with me! What could be better than that?

"And, I was going to save this until after we talked to your mom, but now seems like a good time." Carl pulled out a small box and envelope.

"What's all this? Late birthday present?" I eyed him suspiciously and opened the envelope first. Inside was an admissions letter to attend Puget Sound University and the tuition was paid for by Vamp Modeling Inc.

"Are you serious?"

"Call it a little restitution. I hear they have a pretty impressive art program."

I didn't know what to say. I was going to college to study art. Like I always wanted. I looked at the box and opened it cautiously. A lovely gold ring with a crest stamped on it lay on a blue velvet background. I gasped.

"What's this for?" I took it out carefully, afraid to smudge it.

"It's your vampire license." Carl helped slip it on me and then flashed his own ring. I noticed they matched.

"I can't believe you're coming home with me and I get to go to school. You know, I couldn't have made it this summer without you." I was serious. Carl literally saved me.

"You would have managed, Syd. You're a fighter and, after all, you *are* armed with Fendi and Ferragamo."

"Hmmm." I sighed blissfully, squeezing his hand. "Fendi, Ferragamo, and fangs. Who'd have thought it's what models were wearing this season?"

Interviews with the Vamps

Olivia's Interview

1. So, are you okay with being a vamp now?

Wow, that's a really hard question. I mean, I guess what you're asking is if I'd do it over again, and my answer to that is no. Because, you know, I only did it in the first place because I had no choice. Okay, that's totally not true. I mean, I could have just died, right? But I was too scared of that. Now though . . . well, now I guess I'm scared of the whole living forever thing. Once you're staring forever in the face, it's a whole lot more overwhelming than you could imagine beforehand. Trust me on that one.

2. What does your grandmother think of the whole vampire thing?

Ah, um, yeah. Well, I kind of haven't told her. Damien and I ended up in . . . Oh, well, maybe I shouldn't say. Let's just say we're not in Texas. But I called her and told her that I wasn't doing the modeling thing anymore and that I was fine and all that. She said that she was glad I wasn't strutting around anymore. But that's all she said. She never asked where we were, or even *how* we were. Damien's family asked, and we even told Kathy. And although I tried not to be hurt by my grandmother's total and complete disinterest, it was hard. I guess she knew I'd pretty much given up the science thing. Which meant I'd given up turning into my parents. So she gave up on me. Damien says not to worry about it—that he loves me and that's what matters. But it's still hard.

3. So has Damien really forgiven you for becoming a vamp?

Oh, yeah. I mean, I think so. Or, at least, I guess so. Oh, jeez. Now why did you go and ask me that? Give me a second . . .

Yes. Yes, definitely he has. We've had a few rough patches and all, but the bottom line is that we're together. Forever. And by "forever," I mean, well, *forever*.

4. What do you miss most about being a regular teenage girl?

Milkshakes.
Honestly, that pretty much sums it up.

5. Why did you do this interview? After all, isn't the whole vampire thing supposed to be super-secret?

Well, it's not like we vamps come with a rule book or anything. I mean, there were rules at the modeling agency, but if you read my story, you know that I am *so* out of there. Now, I guess, anything goes. But you're right—vamps do keep to themselves. It's because of all that prejudice. You know, blood-sucking fiends and all that. It's really not true! I'm just trying to get by now. But I thought that it was important for other girls to know what happened to me so that they can be careful. But I have to worry about my privacy, too, you know. So just because you're reading this, keep in mind that while everything I say is true, the names have been changed to protect the not-so-innocent-anymore . . .

Veronika's Interview

1. Are you still gaining weight or did you find some fat-free blood?

Sigh. This is still a huge problem for me (no pun intended). Even though I'm now on a strict diet of only low-cal blood, I haven't slimmed down much. I'm starting to think the vamp lifestyle doesn't agree with my metabolism! Thankfully, I've just employed a top-notch personal trainer who forces me to break a sweat five times a week in the gym. I've gotten some great results so far (my waistline is definitely smaller, and so is my ass) although the scale hasn't moved much. But hopefully I'll be back where I was (pre-vamp) in no time.

2. How about Jackson? Is he okay with his new vamp status? Did he ever make another record? Maybe a really vampy one?

Jackson is loving life as a vampire…although he seems not to love me so much these days. Soon after Dex turned him, Jackson hooked up with an insanely hot undead chick named Lola. Jackson released his new album, *Once Bitten*, two months ago. He's taken on more of a Goth look, dying his hair black and cloaking himself in dark clothing. The album has been a huge smash, and Lola's been right there beside him the entire way. I thought Jackson and I were finished for good. But then just last week, he called and said he's been thinking about me. And now we're planning to go for mojitos tomorrow night. I'll let you in on a little secret: I'm thinking about making a play for Jackson, trying to win him back. At first I was intimidated by Lola, but now not so much. Sure, she's gorgeous, but she's nothing more than a hanger-on, a desperate wannabe who's only dating Jackson because he's a star. I can take that little twit. Mark my words.…

2. Do you have any Fendis or Ferragamos? Or are you on to the next big thing?

I have so many Fendis and Ferragamos that I've seriously lost count. And believe me, honey, I was on to the next big thing five minutes ago!

Sydney's Interview

1. Was there any payback from the vampire community after taking down the evil vamps that changed humans without permission?

Now that vampires are all law-afied, changing humans without a license is pretty frowned upon. I mean, it still happens. Don't get me wrong. You can only civilize the undead so much. I am pretty much accepted except I do catch crap for being friends with the gals over at Psi Phi House. A lot of bigotry still around for half-bloods even though they kind of saved the world. Guess some things take longer to change.

2. Are you still modeling?

First of all, modeling is hard work. I mean, I thought it would be a breeze and all because the whole idea of being photographed wearing pretty clothes just sounds like a dream job. Uh, no. On one job they had me in a formal prom dress in the middle of a dairy farm with the hem pulled up practically over my head while wearing those big, rubber boots so I wouldn't sink into all the cow manure. Does that sound glamorous to you? Blech. Nope, I am way over the modeling thing. I'm studying art at PSU and have met other vampires just like me. And, I have a running comic in the school newspaper so life, or lack thereof, is pretty good right now.

3. What do you think of your author, Serena Robar? Is there anything you'd like to say to her about your experience?

I'd have to say I wasn't thrilled to be turned into a blood-sucking freak. However, Serena made Carl way hot and for that I can almost forgive her the whole undead thing. Almost. I have to wonder what kind of mind can think up this kind of stuff. I mean, really, what is going on up there? Was she one of those weird kids who talked to themselves when they thought no one was looking? Does she spend her days obsessing about death and vampires? Or maybe she's just some mom with an overactive imagination who desperately needs to get out of the house once in a while? Who knows? All I can say is I dig my happily ever after, even if she didn't go the traditional route.